THREE SEVENS

THREE SEVENS
A STORY OF ANCIENT INITIATIONS

BY THE PHELONS

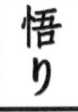

REBEL SATORI PRESS
BAR HARBOR, MAINE

This edition first published in 2010 by
Rebel Satori Press
P.O. Box 363
Hulls Cove, ME 04644

www.rebelsatori.com

Originally published in 1889 by The Hermetic Publishing
Company, Chicago, IL.

Book Design by Sven Davisson

ISBN 978-1-60864-022-5

PREFACE.

Greeting to those who love knowledge and seek understanding, for to them shall come the satisfying of their desires. The things herein written, although they may not seem probable, are possible.

All things, of any and every kind whatsoever, which may enter into the thought of man, can, under favoring circumstances be made manifest. But this is immaterial. We should always regard, not the dress, but the man who wears the dress. So do not linger to question the story clothing the parable.

That which lies within, concerns the truth of being. All the mortal-born travel the same road. The paths are rough and stormy. They drip constantly with the blood of torn and weary feet. Storms brood loweringly along their devious windings. Disasters by flood and fire, enwrap all who dwell upon the earth. Not one would care, even for a short half-hour, to view the misery and suffering that is the lot of those who dwell upon the Earth.

The initiations of the physical, which are to give power, strength and dominion to the Divine Essence, over all the created, visible and invisible are herein typified. In as few words as possible, we have sought to show the common suffering of mortals; from whence they come; whither they go; what they may attain; and that he who seeks can receive, only by uniting the lower self with the Higher Principles, thus becoming one with the Infinite.

We trust they who read, will be quick to see, between the lines, the intended lesson, and that it may lead all into the illumination of the Supreme Truth, that the Divine Unity and Harmony are one, both in Infinity and Eternity.

William P. Phelon, M.D. &
Mira M. Phelon, C.S.B.

CONTENTS.

CHAPTER I.

CHAPTER II.

CHAPTER VI.

CHAPTER VII.

CHAPTER I.

I T HAS ALWAYS BEEN the petted weakness of my family to have ancestors. The pictures and records of said units in the line of descent, are the capital on which the later generations have banked. The dividends have been in almost all cases ridiculously small. In spite of this, because the majority of the united voice of the family and its friends have always persistently declared the profits, we, the minority, have learned to be content therewith. In a humble mood, we take so much as pleases us, of our apportionment of the crusts of dignity and riches thrown at us.

This ancestor-worship may be very nice, in the ordinary unfolding of life. Sometimes, however, one of the said ancestors undertakes to overshadow the life of a younger scion, or perhaps to be that scion. Then the pathway of the overshadowed, through life, is not made any smoother.

In fact, I know this to be my case. Several hundred years ago, one of the grandfathers was a natural mystic. He loved the Invisible more than the Visible. He had eyes to see beyond the veil, and ears to hear the sounds of the "undiscovered country." His portrait, grim and forceful, hangs in the great gallery of that branch of the family who still holds the ancestral lands. In the archives of the Old Hall are written records of his supernatural powers, by which success came to him, in spite of the accidents usually overwhelming common mortals. He was accused by the ignorant of Superhuman knowledge, and an almost total disregard of the orthodox religious practices of that day. But his immense wealth and high position barred to curious outsiders anything but a most superficial notion of his career. He was very near the throne, and at least two reigns were made powerful and brilliant through his direct influence.

There are persons who have studied both his portraits and his character. They assert his description and likeness are mine, in character and feature. According to the best attested tradition, my unfolding corresponds to his unfolding. I cannot truthfully deny being a natural mystic. There is also a consciousness of certain reasons, proving to myself that I am my renowned ancestor. This solves for me, in the affirmative, the question, "Can a man be his own grandfather?"

To the natural mystic, no possible occurrence ever seems impossible. Everything we are conscious of is simply thought made visible. Whatever, then, thought can reach, even in the wildest flights of imagination, may become, under favoring conditions, visible to personal sense. Nothing that thought can grasp, or the human mind conceive, is impossible.

From my earliest recollection, I have been able to see forms, which to others are viewless. Ofttimes, in unfamiliar positions, the real and the unreal appear with equal vividness. When introduced to strangers this embarrasses a little in the matter of salutation, because address to the ordinarily unseen, would give evidence of "crankiness."

In later years, thought, mentally formulated with persistence, becomes an entity to my vision. If to all this be added recurring memories of a life, not the present, in whose scenes the utmost potency of a human will, and that will apparently mine, was projected for purpose, it will be easy for the reader to perceive how tangled has become the identity of my ancestor and myself.

As a child, solitude was always preferable to company, a single congenial friend to a crowd. Sitting passively, the walls of any room where I might be would fade away, and landscapes of tropical fervor and oriental gorgeousness, amidst which I was an honored master, would become, for a moment, a most intense reality.

Never has there come a crisis in my affairs which was not heralded by distinct premonition, and audibly spoken advice, terse and unmistakable, given at the critical moment.

If a great desire has possessed me for the accomplishment of purpose, the potency of my will expressed as intent has brought its realization to me. It mattered not whether it was influence on atmospheric conditions, change of place, or possession. Out of the limitless storehouse of the Astral, all have been granted me, under the conditions of the "manna" to the children of Israel, in the desert: for present use, and the assurance of supply for future needs.

In the later years, obligation for action on certain lines has been strongly laid upon me. I am to Do, to the extent of my ability, neither asking questions, nor formulating doubts. Under this obligation come to my readers these pages. I have done my best, at the point of doing. The invisible purpose will work its own end. It satisfies me to be the link binding the Eternal Past to the Eternal Future.

From the previous statement, no one would be surprised to hear me say, it did not seem strange for me to find myself in the hub of the world's traffic; the city of the incredibly monstrous, London. This dark, noisome sewer smells to heaven. Through it, the crime and blood- guilt of a selfish world has oozed for ages, until the only hope of purification can be by fire. London is no worse than other cities, only in the accumulation of the uncleansed vileness of centuries. Under Karmic law, this piles up like the thunderheads upon the horizon, until a moral cyclone, or a mental thunder-storm restores equilibrium and the light of the Good, by manifestation, brings back the lost harmony.

In another sense, London is worse than other cities, because, from the intense forcefulness of his character, if he becomes a brute, an Englishman is brutal in proportion to his dogged persistence. I do not love London, and am there only when obligation cannot be evaded.

During the period of which I now speak, one day in passing leisurely along a quiet street, just ahead of me an individual attracted my attention, who combined all the exterior marks of age with the vigor and elasticity of youth. Watching him narrowly, for his bearing seemed strangely familiar, the impression so often made upon us came to me, that if the face should turn toward us, it would be that of an acquaintance, or at least one we should recall. At the same time we are absolutely certain we have never seen it before. Indeed, oftentimes, incidents in which we were both actors seem about to be recalled, while we certainly know, in our present lives there has never been any simultaneous action to be transferred to the memory. In this curious condition of my mind, we both came to a standstill on the same crossing. He, a little in advance, seemed introverted, or absent-minded.

As he stepped off the pavement upon the street-level, I glanced around the corner and saw a runaway horse, with pieces of the thills still dangling at his heels, tearing down upon us in such fashion as to make contact with the stranger inevitable. I dashed forward and seizing him by the shoulders, dragged him back just in time to save him a severe blow, if not worse.

As he turned his marvelous face toward me, in the first moment of questioning surprise at the abrupt handling, the flash of his large, dark eye betokened reserve power, awful to contemplate even at its first manifestation. His hair, white, but vigorous and profuse as if he were but twenty, covered a high, broad forehead, and a regular, oval face on which the seal of intellect was stamped in every feature and lineament. This was modified by an expression of kindness which would win the heart of a child at once. Over all this, like a transparent veil, was that appearance which rested on the face of Moses, as he came forth from the Visible Presence. It is the reflection of the light beyond the land and the sea. Once seen and felt, it never fades away. It was plain to me then, why, out of all the hundreds of passers, he only had attracted my inner self to him.

In less time than it has taken to tell, the whole event had happened, and he with stately dignity was courteously acknowledging the favor done him. Handing me his card he pressed me to call upon him at my earliest convenience. Bidding me good day with that peculiar inflection which, like a benediction, always brings a blessing with it, he passed on his way, into the crowd.

He left me dazed and overwhelmed by the weird feeling of meeting a friend I knew had long been dead. Looking at his card I saw an historical name, at one time popular and famous for remarkable powers, but long since withdrawn from public scrutiny. It was, however, well-known to the occult fraternity that he was living in retirement, which no one unbidden might dare to intrude upon. Was it chance or guidance that had thus introduced me to one of the Masters? We shall see, and also why he dwelt within the confines of a great city like London.

The third day after the adventure which was to mean so much to me, as, in my rooms, I was sitting at my writing table, a letter was laid upon the partly written sheet before me. The door was locked and the windows were closed.

No one in the flesh had entered the room. The missive had come out of the nothingness, which is the somethingness of everything existent. It was folded, and sealed, and directed plainly to myself in a familiar hand-writing.

It contained an order to attend a meeting of the brotherhood, of which I was an affiliated member. Directions and commands had often come to me from the same source, written by the same hand, but permission had never been given me to attend even the exoteric meetings. One of the first maxims impressed upon my memory at the beginning of my occult study was to "wait and learn."

The pleasure of sitting in one of these convocations had often suggested itself to me. That which at the first had been desire, had ceased to be anything but an anticipated pleasure of the future. It is needless to say, the appointment was promptly kept on my part. The happenings of that period are now, with the consent of those in authority, revealed for the first time. Copying from my diary, the record is as follows:

November 3rd, A. M.—A dark, foggy day, even for London. The hour of appointment is seven P. M. I am to be called for. The cabman must be my guide as well, for the locality is a strange one for me. I must be ready promptly."

That which follows was written immediately after the events recorded:

"A few minutes before the hour, the doorbell rang and the servant announced the cab. Throwing on my cloak and cap, I stepped out into the unabated gloom. A casual glance suggested to me that the lights of the cab pierced the blackness with a peculiarly aggressive clearness. There was a weird air of unsubstantiality about the whole conveyance. Upon entering the vehicle a sensation as of a cold wind blowing suddenly against me caused me to shudder. Putting this aside with the explanation that it was one of the latest effects of that horrid fog, it occurred to me that the driver had neither stirred nor spoken. The cab door had closed of its own volition, and we were already in motion at a swift pace. It was now plain to me that there was no sound to the horse's hoofs, no rattle nor jar of wheels on the stony pavement. Turning upon a quiet side street, the fact was confirmed that neither sound nor echo marked my rapid transit. I should have been startled, had not, long ago, the mysterious ceased to startle or even surprise me. It was impossible to have any idea of direction or distance. Ahead, shone out a brilliant stream of light, like the headlight of an engine, only whiter and more penetrating. It seemed to carve the large, powerful black horse out of the surrounding darkness. It was more like a dream than a reality.

"At last, in the heart of London, we stopped in one of those country squares accessible only by a court which is 'no thoroughfare.' Originally the residence of a merchant grown rich in trade, the swelling tide of business needs and uses had been limited and held back until the hemmed-in homestead was accessible only by a single narrow alley-like street. Even the greed of avarice had forgotten its location.

"The cab stopped. I stepped through the voluntarily opening door upon the pavement, and turned to the cabman's seat to settle my fare. Nothing was visible but the darkness. Horse, cab and driver had disappeared as utterly as if the earth had swallowed them up, or as if they had vanished into the shadows of a stereopticon dissolving view.

"For a single instant, a dazed sensation of isolation swept across my mental vision. How should I, a stranger, find my destination? The thought had scarcely formulated itself, however, when, on the door of a massive structure looming up before me, flashed out of the darkness with a phosphorescent gleam, the number to which I had been sent. I groped my way up several steps and managed to find the old- fashioned knocker. At its ponderous sound, the door swung open, disclosing a plainly furnished interior. My wrappings were taken by the footman in waiting who then ushered me into a small side room on the first floor. As I entered, a clock, with a far-off sounding chime, struck the hour of seven.

"Undecided, in my own mind, as to the next step, suddenly hands were laid upon my shoulders and a voice whispered in my ear: 'Be silent and obey,' adding a word that had brought to me many occasions for rejoicing. At the same moment a hood was slipped over my head. Blind-folded and pinioned, my shoes were removed from my feet and replaced by slippers, whose contact with the pavement gave back neither sound nor echo.

"My captors conducted me through what seemed a main hall, turning three times, at a right angle each time. At the first turn we descended three steps, at the second five, and at the third seven.

"Here one of my guides gave a signal of three, five and seven knocks upon a door. He was challenged, answer returned, then entering a lift we moved up. At the height of twelve feet came a challenge. The reply being satisfactory, we proceeded. Five times were we challenged. The last time I was asked: 'Who is your Master?' The name was promptly given, and permission was granted to raise my hood.

"I found myself in a room occupying all of the upper floor of the building. The solidly ceiled walls and floor, slightly elliptical in shape, gave no sign of ingress nor egress. Standing in a circle about me were fourteen forms, myself the fifteenth. Long flowing robes of white, and hoods of dark serge completely disguised the identity of each individual.

"He who acted as the presiding officer said in sonorous tones: ' Once again the sacred number is complete. Let no unhallowed foot defile the holy places.' ' As thou hast said, let it be,' answered the rest of the brotherhood.

"The form and bearing of the chief speaker had been often seen by me. There was something in the undulating contour of all his movements that suggested a vanishing point.

"I had, for many years, been the pupil of

a master who had never, as yet, made himself visible to me in the flesh. Good reason had been given me to suppose, during this visit to London the pleasure of an interview with him would be granted. As all this, in sequence, flashed across my brain, a voice reached my inner sense, saying: 'Not here, nor now. Be patient.' I made no farther question, even in thought.

"Looking about me, I noticed there was neither door nor window. The whole circular side and the floor of the Hall were apparently one piece of cedar of Lebanon, dark with age. No sooner had this fact fixed itself upon my perception, than I heard again the voice: 'So incloses the circle of necessity every man born of woman.'

"Overhead, the roof was vaulted in the form of the concave blue above the earth. On it I could see faintly the outlines, in miniature, of the heavens above us.

"'This teaches, that escape from the bondage of matter lies only through the study and perception of that which is above us,' said the voice.

"I looked for the source of light, by which these curious things were visible. There was no candle, gas, nor other human mode of illumination. Everything was, however, perfectly distinct. It seemed like the light of day, but I knew it was night outside, and a dark night at that.

"And the voice said: 'Light is the birthright of all children of the Father, and is free to all. Do you understand?' I bowed assent.

"Then the sonorous accents of the Master, speaking in the outer, said: 'Let the instruction commence by threes.'

"Following two of my companions, who beckoned to me, we moved to reclining seats on couches, which might have been taken from the Hall of a Greek symposium. Thus, half- reclining, our eyes fixed on the starry vault above us, which now flamed out with startling distinctness, the eldest discoursed of the Unity from whence came all things that are. It is impossible for me to recall all his impressive bursts of eloquence. But the following stamped itself most vividly upon my mind:

"'There is but one self-existent force. It is the germ cell of all manifestation. Everything comes forth from It, and everything returns to It. There is but one Truth, and that is the truth of Being. There is but one law, and that is the law of polarity. There is but one motion and that is vibration. All is one. Only in the illusion of manifestation does duality become visible. Aspire always in harmony and alignment with the One.'

"To this instruction, clearly and forcibly stated, each of the members of the triad added what little stock of knowledge was ours. When we reached the point of man's creation, we were arranged in fives, and instruction imparted in the same manner. Finally, when the relations of man to God, and to his environment, were the topic of discourse, we were grouped in sevens, while the Master of the Section, from a raised dais, taught us, as one having authority and wisdom and understanding. Would that the world was ripe for his instruction.

"When he had made an end of speaking, he lifted his hands in benediction. For the time being all memory of self had disappeared. The rising flood-tide of new truth and novel presentation had overwhelmed me. In this condition unconsciousness supervened. With a start I found myself in my bed, at my lodgings. Could it be possible I had dreamed all this? The clock at the foot of my bed indicated days of the week and month. Looking up at the dial the hands stood at November 10. Seven days had elapsed, since, on the open page of my diary, I had noted the incoming of a long-hoped- for day." So closes the record.

A few days after this, in a portion of the city unfamiliar to me, an irresistible guidance rested upon me. To this there can only be submission. It suddenly came into my thought, that the street and number corresponded with my friend's card, whom I had the honor to protect from accident at the street crossing.

The mansion antedated the Elizabethan era. It was built with all the massiveness by which, in constructive operations, our ancestors expressed their haughty pride. The determination to baffle the destroying power of time was evident in every detail. Defiant through age and change have these buildings stood in their impenetrable British obstinacy, until their very stones have become saturated with the darkness and fog of the world's clearing house. On the three-ply oaken door, a big, brazen Egyptian scarabaeus gleamed with as much brightness as was possible to be induced by polishing a London door knocker.

I went up the five, foot-worn steps, and raising the brass beetle let it fall. Perhaps it was my nervousness; or it might have been the stillness of the quiet street, but it really seemed as if the fearfully resonant clang shook the old pile to its foundations. It was out of all proportion to the means employed. The door swung ponderously open, and a servant of oriental face and lineage, with profound salaam, took my card and ushered me into a small waiting-room at the left.

Here, after a very short interval, my chance acquaintance entered. As I rose to greet him, the far-off voice, I have before mentioned as knowing so well, challenged, and I replied. When the pass-words were interchanged, the sound Wended and became one with his own voice, as, offering his hand, he gave me greeting. His face opened in its expression, and I was conscious of standing in the presence of my beloved Master, who, for so many years, had unreservedly offered me all that could be desired of the knowledge of the truth. In the ensuing conversation, he casually expressed himself as having had personal acquaintance with a gentleman of my family, naming my ancestor, of whom I have been so harassingly conscious.

As there is an interim of several hundred years between the time of my ancestor's career and the period now spoken of, to the ordinary routine thinker it would appear, either that there was a strange coincidence, or the old gentleman was a little unbalanced. To me his statement seemed perfectly natural. Recurring memory, to my personal consciousness, sustained the assertion. It never occurred to me, for a single instant, to doubt the fact.

When, after a long and pleasant chat, we separated, the invitation to come again was not simply from the lip. He was evidently satisfied with my progress. Turning to an oleander tree, standing in a little recess, he picked from it a bud just developing from the stalk. Handing it to me he said: "When this shall have bloomed, come again." To all appearance, the chances were a thousand to one that it would dry up and wither away, instead of blooming. Preserving it carefully in my note-book I carried it home, and laid it on my writing table.

On the fourth day, the bud which had in no degree lost the freshness of its first plucking, burst, in an instant, into full bloom. At the moment of its action my eyes were fixed upon it. But I could not describe the occurrence. Without warning of sequence, beyond a slight increase in size, it was only a step from the bud to the fullest bloom.

It was one of the marvels of the Orient, of which travellers tell us so constantly and persistently, while we regard them as bordering closely on the impossible. We listen attentively to our travelled friends, whose words we would believe on any other subject, and wonder how persons with so much sense could be humbugged with such jugglery. We also wonder if they expect us, *wise us,* to be convinced by such thin mendacity of a pilgrim's tale.

As I have said, when the flower came thus into its full expansion, my gaze was fixed upon it. All my surroundings vanished. I was seated on a divan, covered with the richest textures of Indian looms, rare, beautiful and costly. Through the open verandah of a beautiful marble palace, came soft, spice-laden breezes from the rare flowers of the great gardens. Around me was everything that pertained to the cultivation and enjoyment of the sensuous. By my side was a fair girl, upon whose cheek the seal of the tropics was but lightly set. I was her emperor, her king, her light, her life. I could hear her voice, like the ripple of the sad waves, saying:

"But, as my lord goes hence into the changes of the measureless future, when shall Isa see him again? Will he still love her?"

"The bond," I answer, "will always bind, Isa, wherever the soul manifests in a human body, be it man or woman."

"Will my lord swear it to Isa, by the oath that, until redeemed, obligates the soul, for all time to come?"

Resistlessly I hear the slow, solemn words of that awful adjuration, seemingly voiced by myself.

Plucking a full-blown blossom from an oleander, just outside the verandah, she flings it up toward the lofty ceiling. It disappears utterly.

"That shall be our pledge. When, out of the astral currents the blossom comes again to thee, remember, Isa's soul claims love and devotion."

The lines grow misty, and out of the dimness comes back the everyday surroundings. The oleander blossom lies before me still, in its freshest fragrance. Was it really the pledge of that incarnation closed thousands of years since? And who is Isa? Is she—? But I am forbidden to utter that name. Has she, inspired by love, using her powerful intellect and quick perceptions, been able to become a guide and teacher? Love is at once the mystery and the absolute controller of the Universe.

Many things grow perceptible in the light of this lesson. The kaleidoscope of life has turned in a most unexpected manner. But through it all, I feel possessed of the double consciousness of the seer, and do not read it, only as for another.

I have lingered, thinking, but now gladly prepare to obey the summons. It does not take long to reach my destination.

He receives me, this time, in his library, a large room filled from floor to ceiling with books in many languages, a large part in manuscript and cipher. Millions of money would be freely given for the translation of some of these ciphers, for therein was hidden the knowledge that can give health, wealth and potency. He held the key, and was satisfied to be ungorged and unburdened with a load of wealth. The happiness of understanding was his. All physical elements and conditions were under control. Master of the secrets of the Universe, he had no desire beyond the utmost frugality of habit. Attainment destroys desire.

Of the purport of our conversation, and the instruction received then, and at succeeding occasions of my intimacy with him, it is not a part of this story. In the visible we became the closest of friends, as we had always been whenever, in previous incarnations, we had met.

To all outward appearance, my friend was a person who lived in retirement, on ample means, absorbed in abstruse studies. When he first came to London, he had been a practicing physician. He still had a few wealthy patients, who were able and willing to pay the fees he demanded in hopes of shaking off their patronage altogether. It must be confessed his patients were seldom sick.

Passing thus lightly over these details, necessary to the understanding of the story, we come to the point where this story really commences. It is his story, not mine, I am trying to tell.

CHAPTER II.

I T WAS AGAIN NOVEMBER. A short year it had seemed to me. So wrapped into and aligned with his had my life become, that a similarity of both desire and expression was constantly manifesting itself. All my spare time was spent with him, and he had permitted me the honor of assisting him in some of his experiments, which have brought much help to a world unconscious of their origin or results.

He invited me to spend his birthday with him, much to my own delectation, for I had no expectation of being anything to him but a foil for his own thoughts. It was a day impossible anywhere under heaven, save in London. Dark, drizzly, chilly and gloomy, it would, without effort, lead the wise to stay indoors, if possible.

For the first time, I had been admitted into his *sanctum sanctorum,* a room opening out of his large laboratory. From this, all influence or currents that would jar with his, even in the shadow of a vibration, were scrupulously excluded. Here retiring into the silence, he was in touch with the Universe. To this as a center, the vibrating currents, like invisible threads bound to him, alike the known and the unknown, of all ages and climes. The slightest jar of inharmony would have disarranged and shaken off some of these sensitive agents. He, being in perfect harmony with himself, had no fear. But he who entered into the holy place with him must also be one with him, as he was one with the Universe. It is a law of which mankind understands but little. Comprehending this, I fully appreciated the honor he tendered me.

The room was solidly ceiled with a dark, fragrant wood, capable of receiving a high polish. Each of the three sides seemed a single piece, so perfect was the cunning of the builder. The gloss of the richly-veined surface, dark with age, was simply superb. The door through which we had entered, fitted so accurately, as to show no joint, and moved by a secret spring. On the fourth side was a fire-place and a mantel. Resting upon this, flashing in the fitful firelight, were specimens of gold and precious stones, as they came from their original resting places, whose value would have paid a king's ransom. The floor was of polished cedar of Lebanon, as carefully joined and burnished as were the sides. Costly rugs were carelessly spread. Across one side ran a divan, on whose cushions we rested in the Eastern style.

Golden salvers, bearing delicate sweetmeats and rare fruits, were placed before us by the invisible ones, who will always obey those who know how to control. From the center of the ceiling hung a quaintly-carved, solid, crystal vase, from which a soft, clear light overflowed and filled the room. "One of my inventions," my host smilingly said.

It was late in the afternoon, or rather early in the evening, when we were served with Oriental hookahs, and a bottle of what seemed to me very rare, old wine. To this day, however, I do not know whether it was wine or some other subtle elixir.

Throughout the whole repast, my Master partook sparingly, and as we sat with the dessert before us, although it was unalloyed with the usual grossness of human feasts, he seemed to have little desire or use for it. The quiet gravity of his face, in its depths of repose, was overspread with his manifested love for me, whom he had so honored.

We had been chatting in low tones, thinking of many things, both in the visible and the invisible. I noticed, as if my attention had been suddenly called to it, a curiously formed ring, worn upon the little finger of his left hand. It resembled a crown of golden thorns inclosing a garnet of blood-red hue, upon which was engraved a word in oriental characters, Sanscrit, I think. Several times, as I had looked at it during the afternoon, something, best described as a flowing current, pulsated beneath the surface, bringing a little awesome shiver to the spectator. It was as if the vital current of the wearer had here come into sight, beneath the transparent, polished surface, as the arterial blood moved towards the heart.

Now, as we reclined in silence, a feeling of peace, and entire harmony with the whole Universe, stole over me. It was the lullaby of the Great Mother—who giveth rest to those who will yield themselves to her. In this semi- trance state of self-abnegation, as my attention was called to the ring, a corruscation of light shot out from the word on the stone. His hand laid carelessly upon the cushions of the divan, in such a position that the projected ray fell upon the shining surface of the wall at right angles to us. It resembled the gleam of a stereopticon, only clearer and more penetrating. Within this light, like a scene shone upon, not reflected, came a picture.

It was the palace I had once before seen. Outside, the prince's mounted suite, and a single richly-caparisoned Arabian steed, with empty saddle, waited the chieftan's order. Within, the prince, bidding Isa farewell, is receiving from her a jewel set in gold, and attached to a gold chain she takes from about her neck. I see the jewel plainly. It is a blood-red garnet. As he bends over her, I hear plainly, as if her spoken word:

"Generations of wisdom are held within this amulet, my lord; as thou dost wear and keep it, so shall fortune dwell with thee."

"Thanks. So long as I keep it through all the

incarnations, I shall not be content, if thou dost not receive thy portion, whether manifesting or unmanifesting. Love is God, and dies not. If our souls are one, how can we be separated?"

Once more she speaks: "Through the potency of the will, our path through the unnumbered centuries shall never diverge, but shall be ever aligned. To you, the master, shall be honor and place; while I shall be content to learn at your feet."

The picture faded. Curiously, I glanced at the Master. In the peculiar, penetrating pitch, so far-reaching and yet so still, came the voice of his spirit, speaking to my inner sense. The intonation was his own, suave, smooth English, with a slight Castilian accent:

"Senor, perhaps you would know something of my history, which, you already perceive, is so strangely and strongly entwined with yours."

"Nothing would give me greater pleasure, if agreeable to you," Was my reply.

"The hour has come for utterance. I speak, because you can understand. You have often been tried and found worthy to know. Listen.

"Master of self in former lives, I choose to re-enter my present condition, as a Spaniard of noble lineage. In my young manhood, the softness of luxury brought temptation. I loved with all the fervor of Southern blood, forgetting the Past, and unmindful of the Future. I also forgot the precept of warning: that even great ones fall back from the threshold. I had a rival. Mad with jealousy, I slew him in so- called honorable combat. But when his spirit yielded up its body, and his unfulfilled Karma was transferred to my own spirit, forever, my tardy memory came back to me. She for whom the deed was done was not worthy of the sacrifice.

"Overburdened by the upbraidings of my higher self, on whom lay the duty of purifying my blood-stained soul, I eagerly seized an opportunity for expiation. De Soto was fitting out his expedition to search for the fountain of perpetual youth. A young man of 25 years, I entered his service. My unceasing desire for continuous activity, if, perchance, I might escape the lash of my unseen tormentor, or, at least, mitigate its force, was mistaken for enthusiasm. I was praised for the manifestation of the impulse which leads young blood to undergo all manner of privations for the sake of adventure. I did not undertake to explain the true cause.

"Among the heirlooms of our house, said to have been brought by its founder from the far East, was a locket, containing the stone now in this ring. After the fashion of the Orient, it was attached to a heavy gold chain of exquisite workmanship. In my farewell to my father, he gave the jewel into my keeping, because, being the eldest son of the house, legend had determined this entailment to be the proper line of transmission. He bade me always wear it. If I did not, harm might come to me. I wore it constantly, the locket resting over my heart. At that time, however, for some reason unknown to me, its brilliancy was dimmed. The difference between then and now, was the difference between the dead and the living."

Here he paused: the word of power on the stone blazed forth. Within the light on the wall, Spanish galleons were visible sailing on a Southern sea. Approaching a thinly inhabited foreign shore, a band of soldiers left their ships, and by weary marches penetrated the interior to the border of a great river, where they halted. Their leader, whose undaunted spirit, thus far, had surmounted all obstacles, succumbs to the miasmatic climate. With all the solemnity of the last sad rites ordained by the Catholic Church, his body was committed to the embrace of the waters. He had found for himself the fountain of perpetual youth. Here the picture fades, and once more the Master speaks as before:

"So it happened, when we had reached the great river of the West, and De Soto was laid beneath its waters. We landed on the west bank of the river for rest, consultation and refreshment. An attack was made upon us by hostile tribes. Many of our number were killed by our justly incensed and merciless foes. My comrades left me, terribly wounded, as dead upon the field. Our conquerors stripped the slain. While doing this, they found the amulet upon my person.

"An exclamation of intense surprise escaped their lips. A consultation followed. Ascertaining me to be yet alive, my wounds were skillfully bandaged with the healing leaves of some tree, fastened with grasses. Then placing me upon a litter, they bore me by easy stages to a native village among the foothills of a range of mountains. Here I was nursed back to health and vigor. My amulet has never been taken from me. It seemed continually as if courage and strength to endure flowed in an unremitting current directly from it to me.

"When I grew stronger and able to help myself, the chief of the tribe came to me with an interpreter. They told me the Rules of the Order prohibited my dwelling amongst them, because I was of a different race.

"So, as soon as I was sufficiently recovered to endure the journey, they gave me a good horse and asked me to choose whether I would go East to friends, or West to brothers. Seeking only escape from myself, and hoping thus to expiate my crime, my choice was made for the West.

"My decision thus made, an escort of mounted warriors attended me during a two months' journey to the high mountains of the Southwest. Our journey was made easy by short stages, and frequent rests. Of its length, its direction, or its outcome, I cared nothing. The country, over which we passed, interested me slightly. Its extent surprised me, as did the marvelous skill of my guides, who made their way correctly through a trackless wilderness, without a chart or compass.

"Wearied somewhat with journeying, but very much improved in bodily condition by the life-giving air of the mountains, and the constant exercise, oⁱⁱ the evening of a beautiful day, we found before us a rocky barrier. During the whole of the previous day we had been ascending the foothills, but now, the seemingly insurmountable raised its walls heaven high, from the little plateau on which we lay encamped. To the ordinary observer, all further advance was cut off. What next? My escort had so far kept faith with me. I felt sure that there must be a controlling though unseen force behind them, which I could trust to the uttermost. Eo disquieting thought so influenced as to bar sleep.

"At midnight, awakened from a dreamless slumber, I found myself blindfolded and pinioned. A voice, in purest Castilian said:

"'Have no fear! Obey!'

"Surprised to hear my native language in this wilderness, I yielded to guidance. Moreover, I was sure that resistance would be as useless, as my blood-stained life could be for the accomplishment of purpose.

"Led silently along, the cool, fresh mountain air changed to that of confined space. After many windings and turnings, ascents and descents, the bonds were removed. I found myself in a large room, hewn from the rocks. The floor was carpeted with woven fabrics, while rugs of Tyrian dyes covered the divan. A white-robed figure of elegant form, his head and face muffled in the head-dress of an Egyptian priest, bowed to me, and pointing to the divan, said:

"'Be at ease until the morning dawns. Recompense and mercy are even for thee also.'

"Tired with the long march; quieted by the appearance and voice of the priest, I flung myself upon the divan and slept.

"On my awaking, the sun was streaming through a pillared cloister, into which the room I occupied opened. A sensation of relief, unknown since the hour of the fatal duel, possessed me. No longer did I feel that reckless bravado which dares any fate; but humbly resigned myself to the conditions which might be necessary to expiate my crime.

"Presently, attendants waited upon me, and I was allowed the intense satisfaction of a bath, and such toilet appliances as had been strange to me since my farewell to beautiful Spain. It was a little startling that here, in the unknown regions of the earth, a civilization similar to ours, should thus manifest itself.

"After ablutions, and clean garments, my fast was broken by a tray bearing ripe fruits, delicious white bread and honey. When I had eaten, and the attendants had withdrawn, he who had left his benison with me the night before, came once more.

"Addressing me in my native tongue, he said:

"'Senor ———, you are welcome whither you have come.'

"Astounded, for he had called me by my name, in a dazed manner I returned his gravely courteous salutation.

"'Will the illustrious Senor inform his servant how he knew him?' I questioned.

"'All persons and things in the environment are visible to the spiritual sense of sight. He only is blind who fails to perceive. Especially do we watch those who are entitled by merit or lineage to wear the jewel that is yours.'

"'Then it is to that I owe all my good fortune, in being so kindly received by those I supposed to be enemies?'

"'*Si*, Senor. You are protected by inheritance now, but some day we trust you will brighten the lineage of your descent, by winning for yourself a name as illustrious as did the first visible wearer of the symbol.'

"As he spoke I was irresistibly drawn toward him. The sweetness of his tones, the evident sincerity and kindness of purpose in his words, strangely and deeply affected me. Murmuring my thanks, I simply waited further expression.

"'You will wait with us twenty-one days. During that time, you shall have perfect freedom. I shall be glad to attend you. You will not see our faces, until such time as you have chosen either to stay with us or to return whence you came. Nor are you to seek aught that seems denied you. Do you assent?'

"Had there been a thousand ways, no thought except compliance would have been held by me for a single instant. Little knew I then that the great gate of the arcane knowledge was once more slowly swinging open before my feeble, tottering footsteps. This is the gate that swings inward, and never outward. Steps taken, in any incarnation, can never be retraced, even should such a desire, at any time, exist.

"The quick repose of this enchanted spot was marvelous, beyond description. Standing thus isolated in the midst of the wildest and most barren country, the inharmony of its original conditions with man's needs, had been entirely overcome in the interior, while the exterior was still wild and untamed.

"The room assigned me, opened upon a long colonnade, whose roof was supported by a row of columns, both roof and columns having been hewn out of the solid rock. The pillars were square, resting on immense cubic plinths, and the architraves were the lotus of Egypt. A wide flight of easy steps, also hewn out of the rock, descended upon a broad plateau, that might, in former ages, have been the crater of a mighty volcano. Now it bloomed and fruited all the year through, with all the verdure and product of skilled husbandry. The gardens were of wonderful area, considering their location, and through them led a long avenue bordered by stone sphinxes. At one side a deep pool boiled and bubbled constantly, as its waters, fed by an underground stream, rushed into the outer air, and, led into a network of canals, made the luxuriant vegetation of this Eden possible.

"Facing these grounds for a third of the space, stood the vast facade of the rock temple whose interior within the mountain was now my shelter and protection. The rough designing of Nature, man's art, resulting from spirit dominance over his environment, had improved, enlarged and adapted to his own use and convenience, in every instance making the utmost of that which had been furnished to his hand. An impenetrable, rocky barrier protected the outer wall, itself perpendicular and barren on the outside, from the intrusion of the profane. No sign gave hint to prying eyes of the improvements within. The inner wall faced the West. Behind it, towering height above height, the mighty snow-covered peaks reddened in the setting sun, and glistened in the first beams of the light from the East. All danger from avalanches was prevented by a tremendous rift or canon, between our own boundary and the nearest mountain line.

"The immense temple was magnificent in design and execution. For what purpose it had been built, or why it had been located in these stupendous solitudes, I did not then inquire. A new thought had rested upon me. A new inspiration pervaded my whole being. The possibility of expiation. The sense of the surcease of the storm hitherto raging within my breast, made the days pass quickly.

"My companion came to me daily. Our talks were wholly of the unseen forces and their products, or manifestations, which make up the sum total of all the reality of existence. New ideas, and new thoughts suggesting the fancy of recalled memories of long forgotten knowledge, came forth under his skillful promptings, so gravely, sweetly and courteously made. It was like the skilled fingers of a musician touching lightly the keys of an instrument. The echoes of the harmony crowd a full lifetime into a short space. As in the tropics, bud, leaf, flower and fruit follow in quick succession, so my soul, prepared by previous discipline, both mental and physical, yielded readily to the conclusions pressed upon me. As if I had been lost, I found myself again.

"It was the seventh day; the high peaks were still roseate in the fading light. My mentor entered my chamber.

"'My son,' said he, 'I am glad you are so ready

to take up the broken links of the past lives; so willing to be guided by garnered experience. You have not questioned of the future, nor of the past. For your encouragement, in time of trial, yet in the future, behold from whence you came.'

"He had been looking fixedly at me as he spoke. The outlines of the snow-clad peaks towering in the clear air, grew fainter and fainter to my vision. It seemed as if miles and miles intervened. Then another, and totally different, scene spread before my gaze. On a great plain, an immense city unrolled its boundaries. Beyond this city was a palace, mourning and desolation. A noble queen weeps and laments for the loss of her lord, slain upon the battle-field, and now awaiting the last sad honors earth may tender.

"The queen sitting alone, murmurs: 'He died, as a brave man should, defending his patrimony and his people's rights; but to me, by special messenger, with his last breath, did he return the link of the ages.'

"She took from her bosom, the blood-red garnet, in setting and hanging, the *facsimile* of mine. Was it mine?

"She bows over the casket of the soul, now useless and helpless, and a great sob wells up. She grieves for the loss of companionship. The soul who goes hence, like the traveler to foreign countries, is absorbed by the newness of his immediate surroundings and conditions, to the partial exclusion of past connections and associations. It is this that we, the mortal races, all mourn. It is our right to mourn our own loss. We would not bring back to the calamities of the earth-life, not for a single hour, those who have gone happily hence.

"She raises her head. Out of the astral current are borne words of hope for the future. Once again she utters, under her breath, words as if in answer to the far-off promptings:

"'Yes, I know. Generations hence, I shall have the pleasure of re-union, and shall be so re-embodied, that nothing shall prevent the clinging of soul in perfect alignment of thought and purpose.'

"Overwhelmed by the immensity of the future as measured by mortal conception, she bows her head on the bier before her. I see formulated out of the nothingness a shape distinct in feature, shadowy in outline. So intense was the impression, that its remembrance has never faded away. The shadow bends its head and speaks to her. So absorbed have I become, that I hear his words:

"'Mourn not for the dead, Isa, but for the living. Compensation is the law of nature. Let the talisman guide thee on thy way, through the trackless ages of thy destiny, and keep thee humble, as the servant of the One. Blessed shall he be to whom it shall come, if he shall choose the right-hand path, prizing wisdom before aught else.'

"She raises her face. It is the face of one who overcometh, transfigured and glorified. The picture fades. The enormous peaks still sentinel the Temple. My instructor bows gravely and goes quietly out. I lie still thinking until the dawn breaks.

"Three questions present themselves prominently for solution: First:— What chasm have the centuries bridged for me? Second:— How far am I responsible as keeper of the amulet? Third:— What mystery does the near future hold for me?

"As the day broadened, I slept. When the sun was high in the heavens, self-consciousness came to me once more. A new burden of responsibility had, in some strange way, been laid upon me. I was henceforth to live as the culmination of cycles of existence, and not simply as the creature of a day. Moreover, I was to be the guardian and keeper of power transferred, potency to be still farther segregated and transferred. Thus thinking, I took the amulet from its resting place, and was astonished to see that its dull grayness had begun to brighten, just as coming dawn lifts the shadows of the early day.

"My mentor joined me again at sunset, as usual. I especially remember his saying, in reply to a question of mine:

"'My son, there is but one existence, of

which we are all parts, and one purpose and that is the Good. Could there be two, all harmony of manifestation must disappear. Chaos would impend from the moment of divergence. Spirit gathers power from its anchorage to the physical organism. The perfect alignment of the individual to the All, strengthens the individual and gives force and potency to the manifestation of the One. The eye and the hand are part of the whole body. When they are trained, although they are the eye and the hand still, they are of more use to the whole body, in proportion to their trained skill.'

"More swiftly, if possible, went the days and nights. On the evening of the fourteenth day, my friend, as he arose to leave me, lifted his hand in benediction, saying:

"'Let the night be good to thee.'

"And left me with myself. It was the ninth hour. In spite of my own will, my thoughts were dwelling persistently along the track of my family, its standing, its reputation, its traditions, and at last seemed to center on my ancestor, the founder of the house, from whom in direct line of descent, the amulet had come to me.

"As my thought rested more and more fully upon him, I heard a distant voice calling me by name. So far off, it sounded only as the murmur of the sea shell. But my thought had become so concentered, that I listened eagerly.

"Again came the call; this time so intense, so far reaching, that my whole astral self sprang forward to obey its behest.

"Once more the call, more imperative, more absolute. Freed from the bonds of the physical, for a single instant I was conscious of my body lying useless beneath me; while drawn as iron to a magnet, I followed from space to space, a shining silver thread, the power of a potent will.

"At last, kneeling before him whom I knew to be my ancestor, I asked:

"'Who am I, that thou shouldst thus call me from the planes of the lower consciousness?'

"Lifting me to my feet he graciously responded:

"'Thou hast been my pupil ever since thou didst first essay thy flight out of the Divine light into the dark abysses of the natural conditions. When, in the earth planes, thou hast needed my help, I have ever been thy guardian and protector. When, in Devachan, thou hast sought escape from the continual toil of the lives, I, on the lower planes, have maintained for thee such conditions and place, as were necessary. The amulet is the link that binds us, never to be broken. When, in Delhi, first, you were ready to receive it, it was given you by the inspiration of love, through whose potency it could be most efficacious. Thou didst gratefully receive and carefully guard it. When thou didst yield up thy earth-form seeking better conditions for thy progress, I placed it in safe keeping for thee. It has come back to thee. In spite of thy one crime, thou hast been guided to the point where thy true life-work commences.

"'Thou dost now stand where, unless thou shalt forswear all thy former lives, the Universe lies before thee. I have summoned thee thus, to the planes of the higher consciousness, because I have no desire to approach the erratic conditions, from which I am freed. I am about to entrust thy guidance to another, after thou shalt have pledged to me thy word, hitherto never broken, to press forward, until, all obstacles removed, thou shalt attain.'

"As he ceased speaking, he placed his hand upon my head. For an instant the threads of a thousand lives were joined. I saw how, in the past, my spirit had struggled to train its soul for this purpose and condition so rapidly approaching me. The set purpose of all my lives, indelibly impressed itself upon the astral. Never again was it to be put aside. Aspiration and endurance, purpose and potency, had crystallized for accomplishment.

"Again my ancestor's voice sounded plainly:

"'You perceive the beginning and the end. Do you fear to undertake the journey?'

"With not a single tremor of spirit, I replied:

"'I do not fear.'

"'Love, mercy and justice are the pillars of the Universe. Are you ready to offer to each its appropriate sacrifice?'

"'I offer justice ransom, even to the utmost reckoning. Love and mercy as I shall be worthy.'

"'Why do you do this?'

"'Because, all worlds are made better, when one individual atom is made better. What though I perish, if the millions are in the least comforted?'

"'Thou hast answered well. Wilt thou confirm by the oath of a Chela, thy intention to give thyself no rest, until thou canst, at will, seek me here?'

"Without the slightest mental reservation or equivocation whatever, I bowed my head in assent.

"Syllable by syllable, from the lips of my greatest grandsire, impressing themselves like liquid fire on my soul, came the words of that bond, which reaches through all time and space, and is coordinate with Infinite and Eternity, the only dimensions of the Causeless Cause.

"Undaunted and unquailing, I repeated the awful formula after him.

"'Thou hast one more step to take, before thou art ready to discover the way. Trust fully those into whose keeping thou hast come. Thou art to them, even as to me, most precious. Seek to know the One. When thou canst read the word on thy amulet, I shall see thee again. Farewell.'

"A sensation of sinking and giddiness, and I awaken on my divan, not fully conscious, even then, of the full meaning and intent of this interview. But a mighty spirit purpose inspired me, and my whole nature began to assert itself for action on the high lines of being.

CHAPTER III.

REMEMBERING THAT STILL another week was needed to finish the bound set by my friend of the Temple, I lie calm and quiet in the cool of the morning. The daylight breaks over the distant peaks. My spirit lifts itself toward the Eternal, and in aspiration I become one with the Infinite.

"For a third time the days and the nights numbered seven. As my friend leaves my presence for the night, he says:

"'Tomorrow thou mayest see my face if'—

"The suggestion cuts me to the heart. Suppose I should not. It was wonderful how the strong, Spanish pride of my mentality had yielded itself to a most docile affection for this man, whose face I had never yet seen.

"Why should I not see him again? What unseen force or conditions could possibly prevent me? Then came the resolution: 'I will not be prevented. Whatever lies before me, I will meet bravely and fearlessly.'

"The hours move on. The full moon has

climbed to the zenith. Lights and shadows are thrown out with that startling contrast, peculiar to the tropical moonlight. My attention is drawn to a far-off star, how, I cannot explain, but I am fascinated by it. My gaze is fixed persistently upon it. Its rays fill my whole apartment to the exclusion of all other light. As I wonder at the power thus manifesting, the luminous matter concentrates and grows brighter. At the center, a figure shapes itself. As if I saw myself in a mirror, so becomes this to me. Striking and distinct in projection, in outline and proportion a very Apollo, it still seems pale and wan. It tears from its breast its flowing robe, and I perceive an ugly stab in a vital part. I start to my feet.

"'Who art thou?' I ask.

"' I am thy higher consciousness. Thou dost stand face to face with thine own soul. Thou hast sore wounded me. For what thou hast done to me, art thou willing to serve another's good seven-fold, until my wound be healed?'

"Firmly I answer, 'I am willing and eager to begin.'

"'It is well. From henceforth the burden I have hitherto been forced to carry, is transferred to thy lower consciousness, where it shall be carried, until expiation is finished.'

"For the first time in my life, I hear, like an echo from these thrilling words, music from out the manifestation of creative thought. My burden is lighter and my sleep deepens.

"Refreshed, as the new day comes in, I awaken to all which may come. Before the shadows return again, my friend comes to me.

"'It is well with thee!' he exclaims. 'With the gladness of a great joy, I welcome thee at the outer gate of the mysteries.'

"He turned toward me. The veil fell away from his features, and this was the picture: A grave-visaged, calm face, high and broad as to the forehead; piercing as to the deep-blue eyes—eyes restful and quiet now, but full of conscious power. The whole face told of a battle long since fought and won. A battle in which the rightful ruler had warred upon and overthrown the usurper. The successful termination of this inevitable battle of the ages, was broadly defined with ineffable peace. Every line of his whole features was glorified by the impress of the maxim of the wise in all ages : 'To know, to dare, to do, and to keep silent.' It was such a face, loving, tender, true and potent, as artists, whose clear vision perceives beyond the flesh, are wont to give the 'Perfect Man,' who, through suffering unparalleled, illustrates the path, in which all who desire to attain must also walk.

"It was not possible from his face to judge of his age. There was no sign of withering nor shrinking in the flesh. All the lineaments were full and firm of texture, and the glow of matured youth pervaded the whole. It was a face full of expectation instead of memory, of power, not palsy. Pervading all, governing all, was the peaceful calm of invincible purpose and perfected accomplishment, a staying upon the power of the Infinite. Indeed, the perfect soul shone through the windows of the perfected body. It was an organism to which death was now the servant and not a terrifying master. It was an example of what all mankind are privileged to become if they will, perfect souls in perfect bodies. It was fully apparent that he walked constantly in the overshadowing glory of the heavens.

"His benison falls upon me as does sleep upon a tired child. He sits with me talking of various matters. Bye-and-bye, as the moon rises, he bids me farewell, saying:

"'At midnight expect me.'

"I sleep. As the long hours come, I am aroused by a light touch upon my shoulder. To me, broad awake at once, my friend says gently:

"'Come!'

"Two attendants stand beside him, bearing vestments like my friend's; these I assume. When I am clothed, he says:

"'Allow yourself once more to be blindfolded.' Thus muffled I am conducted by devious ways into the heart of the mountain temple.

"When the bandage was removed from my eyes, I found myself in a circular hall, with a flat floor, so hewn out of the solid rock that it was a perfect hemisphere. The diameter was an exact divisor of the earth's diameter. Within the circumference, was traced upon the floor, an ellipse. At one of the foci was a throne or royal seat. At the other an altar, hewn out in a single piece, from the original rock that had once filled the whole space. Upon this altar an unquenchable fire ever burned, sometimes leaping high and strong, and sometimes dwindling down into a slender tongue of flame, more like the flash of a small electric spark. It was the measure of the thought-force of the Brotherhood present. As it flamed up, swayed and concentrated itself, it was an indicator of the potency of projection of their own individuality into the astral currents of the Universe.

"These, and other details, I give from after knowledge, for I did not then perceive nor know them in all their fulness.

"The hall was lighted so that all things within it were plainly perceptible, but from whence the light came could not be cognized by personal sense. On the half ellipse surrounding the throne, were fifteen seats, seven on each side of one placed on the pole of the major diameter. All were of elaborate pattern. Each differed from the others, owing to the idiosyncrasy of the occupant, whose inner thoughts had fashioned them, both in device and construction. But all were similar in the impression they gave of restfulness and content; as if the builder of each had entered into the Great Peace.

"The seat at the end of the major axis was a little broader and higher, indicating deserved honor, but in no sense separateness. The seven seats on either hand equidistant from each other, completed the sum of the three, five and seven.

"The walls and roof were bare. Composed of some kind of porphyritic rock, they were polished like a mirror. The door through which I had entered had moved noiselessly back to its place. No seam nor joining gave hint of its existence. As I looked upon the walls, I was, with all my self-control, startled. They did not reflect a single item of the interior, and yet shadowy outlines flitted constantly across their surface; outlines which my untrained vision failed to recognize.

"At the moment of being unblinded, the occupants of each seat were standing, each by his particular resting place, save one at the right of the Center. They were all habited like my guide and myself. Their faces and bearing were simply indescribable. Nowhere else on earth could be found a counterpart. It was evident that the hands of each were on the latch of the Gates of Gold, simply waiting completion of labor. And the Elder Brother, no artistic thought in beau ideal has ever approached the conception of his perfection; of the return into the original majesty and beauty of Creative Thought, before its manifestation was marred by man's interference, permitted for purpose.

"As my vision became accustomed to the piercing clearness of the light, my guide, making some sign to the Elder Brother, crossed over to the vacant seat, where he stood as did the others, thus leaving me standing by myself, at the foot of the throne.

"The light on the altar flamed and flickered, not as if in any sense enfeebled, but as if swept over by a draught of air. In this hall no such thing was possible, and the movement must have had some other cause.

"Low, musical, but wonderfully penetrating, came words to me from the Elder Brother:

"'Stranger, stand erect! The mighty voice of our unseen brother speaks to us by you, his lawful messenger. Your claim from us is just, not only because you are his descendant, but because you of your own self have proved that fear does not control you. To bravery, you add natural adaptation, and the culture necessary for advancement. You have successfully endured the preliminary trials. It is not too late to draw back. If you choose, you shall go safely and quickly unto your own people. But, if you take one more step, you pass the threshold of the great gate, that swings ever inward, and never outward. This once passed, retreat is impossible, and advancement must be constantly made. Look to the wall on your right.'

"I looked. Out of the mirrored distance, I could discern the links of my own memory—incidents of the beginning of my faintest recollection, and then, in unraveling coil, all my actions, even the minutest, revealed themselves to my gaze.

"As the sequence reached the point of my present *status,* a cloud enshadowed the whole. Out beyond the wavy outlines, a bright light shone, and the flame on the altar leaped up triumphantly.

"'Thou seest the past,' continued the Elder Brother, 'the future is thine own to make. If thou art guided by the lessons of the finished it is well. If thou wilt still, of thine own free will, go on to the irrevocable, advance three steps, and kneel at the foot of the throne.'

"Without hesitation, fearlessly and reverently, I advanced and knelt upon the broad lower step.

"'Repeat after me, this thy new name; for thine old one, stained with mortal folly, thou wilt here leave with thy closed past; and then say on, as thou shalt hear.'

"As I commenced the repetition of this most solemn obligation with my new name, the right hand of the invisible occupant of the throne was laid upon my head. The light waned. The flame upon the altar grew concentered and star-like, in intensity. An overwhelming presence, awful in majesty, seemed to fill the room. Behind the brotherhood standing here, in the visible, were rank upon rank of forms shadowing in dim but perfect outline out of the invisible.

"I cannot reveal the vows of an initiate's obligation otherwise than they were taken. Every word burned itself into my memory as if seared with a hot iron. At the concluding words: ' Let my oath be witnessed by you in all ages to come,' the brotherhood, as one, responded: ' We witness your obligation,' and out of the silence, came also a deep, reverberating echo: 'We, also, witness your obligation.' The whole brotherhood, whether in the flesh, or out of it, were witnesses, for such is their custom. The hand was lifted from my head. A feeling of renewed strength and life flushed my veins and tingled through every nerve.

"For a second time, came to my ear, the voice of the Elder Brother, saying: 'You have entered your novitiate. For seven years, the last one of which shall be the year of the preparation, you will pursue your studies with our brother, to whom you were first assigned. Be obedient. Be faithful. Be studious, and we shall gladly confer that which you may desire.'

"The flame upon the altar flashed up, strong, joyful and vigorous. A strain of music, far-off but distinct, filled the vaulted chamber. A sweet, subtle perfume, reached my nostrils, and kneeling still, I lose myself in space.

"When I return to myself, I am lying on the divan in my own apartment. I wonder if it is all a dream. It was too vivid, and the obligation had left too strong an impression. On glancing about the apartment, the white robes of my new dress testify that I have forever renounced the old, and being born again in purpose, desire and intention, am ready to enter on my novitiate.

"Presently my Guru enters. His tender salutation: ' May the day be good to thee, my brother,' arouses within me a new and strong desire for his guidance and approval. Attendants bring fruit, unleavened cakes and honey, and we break fast together. After we had eaten and drank, he said:

"'While we are under the circle of necessity it is meet that we divide the twenty-four hours into three parts: eight hours for labor, eight for meditation and study, and eight for sleep. So you may find occupation in the gardens in the morning hours, and when the day grows old^ I will come to thee until the hours for rest are at hand.' So saying he withdrew.

"It is not necessary to go into the details of those six year* so quiet and uneventful. In the equal balancing of physical labor, not toil, but a happy mean, and soul culture, and rest, my whole being grew, as the 'flower grows upon the still lagoon.' I gave no thought to time, but enjoyed life as never before, in the truest and highest sense.

"One afternoon, as my Guru had finished a magnificent description of the man who perfectly embodied the creative thought, he said:

"'This night finishes six years of your novitiate. To-morrow morning, you will commence your year of preparation. We will break our fast together.' Bidding me good night, he left me.

"Early in the morning, he came again to me, and when our hunger was allayed by the simple and satisfying meal customary, he said:

"'Come with me to my laboratory.' Passing through a long, narrow corridor, we ascended a spiral staircase of forty-five steps, hewn into the solid rock. This brought us into a large, square room, opening upon the outside surface of the mountain by a dormer window, looking West. On the outside, this was high up on the perpendicular face of the cliff, and not discernible, as having any connection with the artificial. On the inside, a huge block of stone, exactly balanced, and moving by a touch of the finger, fitted the opening, and protected from the inclemency of the weather. Seats were cut in niches around the walls, and a divan ran across the whole of one side. In the wall, opposite the divan, was fitted a large, square stone of polished, black marble, seven feet in length and breadth. Inscribed within the square, was a double circle of white marble. Between these two circles, were arranged in regular order, in red porphyry, the signs of the zodiac. At the four corners, also inlaid of the red stone, were a line, a triangle, a right angle and a square.

"In the center of the room stood an altar, like

the one in the Hall of Obligation, but smaller. Rugs covered the seats and divan. At the head of the divan, a shelved niche held a few papyrus rolls, dark with age and use. Close at hand was a large tablet of slate and a stylus of the same material. Nowhere was visible any of the usual furnishing of the ordinary laboratory, such as crucibles, flasks, furnaces or retorts.

"Hardly had this thought framed itself in my mind, when my Guru said: ' In our explorations of Nature's realm, we do not study effects, believing them to be causes. We do not investigate the unreal and changeable, to find out changeless law. The reflection can teach us but little about the substance of the reflection. You have been moving away from the unreal, into the knowledge of the real. Your training has hitherto been a unit, so far as it concerned the trinity of man, body, soul and spirit. But now, you must learn to know more fully, by what right the spirit claims and maintains dominance over all lower planes of manifestation.

"'During your year of preparation, your study will be of the real: of its laws, of the laws of mind, of our relations to those laws, which mankind, as a whole, has so studiously perverted these many years. We do not need to study books, for we may use the repository of all knowledge, even the astral light. Let us begin our day's duties by passing into the Silence.'

"He sat down, and bade me sit beside him. Upon doing so, after a few moments, a train of thought, subtile in reasoning, conclusive in logic and unanswerable in its scope, as to the first principles of manifestation, filled my whole attention. It was told me afterwards, that it was the mental discourse of my brother and teacher. His voice at last aroused me from my abstraction. Coming back to consciousness of the outer, I noticed a single ray of sunlight rested on the altar.

"It would weary you, without cause, to recount, day by day, the occurrences of that most eventful year. Four morning hours were spent in the laboratory. Four hours devoted to the care of my allotment in common with the Brothers, in the gardens of the Temple. Here the action of mental force upon vitalized, physical conditions was studied, that there might be certainty of self-confidence, in our contact with Nature. Four of the closing hours of day were given to social intercourse, whereby the feeling of brotherhood should be more firmly grounded. The remaining eight hours were given to rest, sleep and refreshment.

"With this general outline, I may venture to give you a few well-remembered incidents. My Guru said the study of Mathematics and Geometry was devised to train the mentality in concentration. In language, we sought for smoothness of expression of our thoughts, and in philosophy, we were constantly seeking to identify ourselves with God and with the Universe.

"When he was not engaged with me, he was occupied with the Caballa, from which he declared, knowledge of everything in the Universe -could be obtained, that being at once a key and an encyclopaedia.

"One day, near the time of the full moon of the first month of my tutelage, he, illustrating on his tablet with his stylus as he talked, said:

"'The problems of Geometry were invented by the Masters, to teach the relations of the unseen forces to the visible and the manifested, and not for physical application. In this latter use, they are necessarily wrested from their true office and purpose. Hear the demonstration of the right-angled triangle:

"'The right angle represents the equal balancing of the spiritual and physical forces, so that neither shall bring detriment to the other. The perpendicular stands for the spiritual. The horizontal or physical conditions lie continually along the same plane, never rising above it, nor can it fall below it. Should it do one or the other, it ceases to be horizontal, ceases to be perfect physical. The perpendicular rising out of the physical plane at every point of its progress is constantly changing its position, growing upward, out of, and beyond the physical environment, beneath which it does not penetrate. It meets the physical at the point of contact only. This point, in the seven principles of man, is represented by the astral body. The spiritual in all its upward progress, and the physical in its *status* of rest and quiet, are bound together by the Infinite, Perfect One. This bond is represented by the hypotenuse, which connects the spiritual and physical on the opposite ends of the line. The extreme points of the perpendicular and horizontal coalescing with the extreme points of the hypotenuse, represent body, soul and spirit, which are but manifestations of the Divine power and presence. The hypotenuse is greater than either the perpendicular or the horizontal.

"A square is the symbol of perfection. It has four equal sides, and four equal angles. This makes four equal perfection. That which is perfect must be real, and the real must be the Perfect One. Then the Perfect, Supreme Intelligence is represented by the square described on the hypotenuse. The square described on the perpendicular, shows forth the perfect spiritual, while that on the horizontal stands for the perfect physical. Because manifestation exists as physical, it does not follow that it is imperfect. Consequently, the square of the hypotenuse or Divine Perfect is equal to both the manifestations of Itself, the Perfect Spiritual and the Perfect Physical. Not until they return into itself will their equality each to each be manifest.

"'Furthermore, the Physical, Spiritual and Intelligent are the Triad which would be incomplete if either of the elements was imperfect or wanting. If a side or angle were missing, or if one of the angles was not a right angle, then the conditions would be incomplete. All things must exist as herein named. Then the stated demonstration will also exist. By it, is clearly proven the power and unity of the One, who is, and was, and will be, through all coming cycles.'

"About a month after that he said to me:

"'It is acknowledged by all philosophers, that no matter how our environment changes in form, no element is ever lost. This must be true, for the element is the premordial point, and is a part of the only real substance, the One, and must therefore be self-existent and indestructible. Wise men even, have been satisfied with the correct enunciation of this proposition, not realizing the logical sequence, that all forms which have once existed, and become invisible by the operation of superior force, can, by the exercise of the creative force latent in man, again resume their visible forms. This unused and forgotten force is man's birthright, as the image and likeness of the One.'

"'Can this be demonstrated to personal sense?' was my question.

"'Let us see. Sit quietly, and you shall have proof.' I looked at him, as he sat motionless.

Under the broad band of sunlight, streaming into the room, his majestic face became as immovable and fixed in its lineaments, as if carved in marble. The mighty spirit within looked straight beyond the environment, into the vastness of limitless space. It was the concentration of the potent will. On the rocky floor between us, appeared a yellowish mist, which apparently solidified until a gold Pistole lay before my astonished gaze.

" The stern lines of my teacher's face relaxed; the sight of the present came back, and his kind voice assured me of his return to actual presence.

"'My brother,' said he, 'take up that symbol man so loves and worships that he repudiates and forgets the real for which it stands. Its value is largely a matter of imputation and belief. But, because by mutual agreement, mankind could, by its use, gratify self, they have veiled their perceptions of the true gold of life, consisting in the mastery of the passions, and self-domination. As thou hast seen it come forth, so only can it be created. The dream of juggling pretenders never left the physical plane, in its search after the philosopher's stone, which is the will directed by wisdom and tempered with knowledge. The vibrations of the astral forces hold in solution the essence of all things. Out of this, can be crystallized, by a will in touch, or capable of harmoniously attuning its own vibrations, whatsoever has, at any past time, manifested itself to personal sense, as the formulation of previous thought. Thou canst measure here the true value of gold, where we have neither desire nor use for it.'

Here my host paused in his narrative, and, turning his open hand toward me, displayed therein an antique gold coin. "I have always, since, worn it as a talisman," he said.

As his hand had been lying perfectly still and wide open upon the cushion, since he commenced telling his story, it might seem a mystery how the coin happened to be there.

"Another month went by," he continued. "As the moon approached the full, I felt conscious of a rapid gain in my understanding of the true relations of my real self to the Macrocosm.

"My Guru had been discoursing on man's responsibility for his dominion over, not only himself and his fellows, but also every living organism upon the earth. He maintained that man had rule and dominion over even the wildest beasts, if he chose to cultivate and use it. Not by physical means, not simply by the power of the eye, so much vaunted amongst civilized people, but by the unseen, silent currents, which sway all animated existence. This is proved by the fact that the eye of a coward will not control the feeblest animal. He who constrains in that manner, must be fearless and brave. It is not the eye, but the force behind it that rules.

"As we talked, we were looking out of the

window into the forest. In plain sight, a gaunt jaguar was crouching upon a little clump of trees, waiting the coming of a mountain antelope slowly climbing a rocky path, leading close by the lair of its fierce, hungry enemy.

"'See, oh, my brother!' I exclaimed. 'Certain destruction awaits the antelope.'

"'Possibly not,' replied my Guru. 'You may see an illustration of my words. The antelope will not be harmed.'

"I waited in suspense. The look of projected power passed over my teacher's face. The jaguar stirred not. The antelope passed on its way unhurt, and apparently unconscious of the awful danger it had so narrowly escaped. When it had gone by, the jaguar crept down from its hiding place, and slunk out of sight.

"A short time after this, another incident of the same controlling power, was as fully and strikingly given. A swift messenger was needed for use. Why the usual method of dissolution and re-materialization was not employed, I do not know, as it was no business of mine, but concerned my Guru alone.

"Standing within the embrasure of the rock-bound window, he looked out upon space. Watching him, as one feels the flow of an electric current, so came to my inner sense perception of the impelled power of will in its greatest concentration. The vibrations were strong enough to appeal to the sense of clairaudience. First a hum, then a well defined musical sound, manifested itself. The impression was of a call that could not be resisted. The sound was peculiar and far-reaching, because the direct result of the impulsion of dominant will.

"A few minutes passed. Out of the brightness of a cloudless sky, a speck grew into a bird, and an immense, untamed condor, flying straight as an arrow shot from a bow, alighted on the rocky ledge, at the feet of my teacher.

"He attached to the neck of the motionless monarch of the mountain air, a chain and a packet, in the same manner as carrier-pigeons are used. The condor having thus received his message, poised himself, his great pinions spread, and then the far-off, from whence he came, again received him into itself.

"'If man had not lost the memory of the things that rightfully belong to him,' said my Guru, ' he would never lack helpers nor messengers. He has trusted to the arm of flesh and been overthrown. When will he see that the perfect spirit brings the perfect body, and the two are essential to the perfect man, who was given dominion over the fish of the sea, and over the fowls of the air, and over every living thing that moveth upon the earth? It was not the dominion of physical force, either; for that is the weakest force of the Universe. Why should he have dominion, if he were not to use it?

He will not learn, and still he mourns his weakness. Weakness! His rightful position amongst created intelligences is next to the Infinite.'

"Several days after the affair of the condor, we were discussing the real means by which one man reaches another by argument. ' It is not in any sense,' said my friend, ' a physical change, but a modification through a person's utterances, of soul condition, which we. name conviction. This change pertains entirely to the four principles, which make up the astral body. These in simple and in mass, are volatile and constantly striving to break away from their bondage to the physical. The link that binds the astral body to its physical expression is adaptable, but is not to be handled nor toyed with, without knowledge, lest there happen events that cannot be recalled.

"'We can send another, wearing only his astral body, out into the astral currents. We should, however, first, be perfectly certain, that the power which sends forth is fully able to recall. Otherwise there may be sad remembrances for us, and knowledge gained by awful experience, of currents twisted into cyclones, of gales and cross-currents, and of Karma to undergo, that was not ours, until thus rashly appropriated. But my dear, younger brother, thou hast reached a point where, if thou hast desire to see for thyself the two-fold distinction of the astral and physical body, now is thy time and Opportunity. Look steadfastly upon me.'

"Obeying his command, a strange sensation of quiet and rest crept over me, a shudder, and then a thrill, succeeded by a sense of ease and lightness, a momentary confusion, as when one passes from the darkness into the light. I was conscious of being outside of my body, which, at my side, was lying at ease, to all appearance sleeping. To my inner hearing came the voice of my preceptor:

"'Thou hast passed, temporarily, the change which, when permanent, men call death. The difference is, that thou hast not relinquished thy right to thy body, and can re-enter at thy will, assisted by me. Wait, and I will call a guide for thee.'

"Resisting the impulse to move, my will held the Scin-Laeca, until another astral form, I recognized as a-temple-dweller, joined me. 'If thou hast desire, lay thy hand in his, and formulate thy wish,' were the words distinctly heard. I did as I was bidden. The wish to see my birthplace in far-off Spain, rested heavily on my soul. At the instant, my thought became an entity to myself. I was also conscious of a swift movement Eastward.

"Suddenly we felt our way confronted by a wall of thick darkness. 'That is opposing force, acting blindly, following the simple law of projection,' said my guide, his voice ringing out in bell-like cadence, a quality which distinguishes all astral utterances. 'Wait until I shall inform the Guru.'

"A moment, and his far-off, potent voice commanded: ' Fear not, but move forward, my force is sufficient for you.' No shadow of fear fell upon us, as we plunged into the midst of the darkness. Ages condensed into a second of time. Resistance made against terrible constriction and oppression, but no thought of retreat. A passage is cleft. Brightness and light once more envelope us.

"All this time, I am conscious of the swift moving toward the East. As in a vivid dream, we stand at last in my ancestral Hall. Familiar with the surroundings, I explained various points of interest to my guide. He gravely acknowledged the courtesy, but when I presented him to some of the cavaliers-in-waiting, his eyes smiled, and I noticed they made no response. Now came to my consciousness, a certain air of solemnity, such as proceeds a weighty event in the life of earth.

"Ascending the stairway to my father's apartments, we passed through the doorway. In a dazed sort of condition I noticed that the heavy, oaken doors were closed, and so remained, and the stiff, tapestried curtains, hanging low, gave no sign of our ingress, only as if stirred by a slight wind.

"My father lay on his pallet, pallid and exhausted. His faithful attendants stood near, and also my mother. As she had been dead many years, I was again momentarily confused, but remembering my present condition, I moved to her side, and greeted her. She affectionately returned my greeting. In answer to my question, why she still remained on the Astral plane, she replied:

"' I wait for thy father before passing on to Devachan. But how is this? Are you also free?'

"I told her I was not yet liberated, only let loose for a little while.

"Then as we talked, the extreme moment came to my father. The astral body rising from the physical, before becoming entirely free, discerned us conversing. The physical body, sympathizing in the transport of joy, exclaimed in its last effort:

"'Oh, my dear wife! My son Manuel!'

"My father's astral body joined our group. Inquiries and information passed rapidly. I asked my guide if they could not return with us.

"'When their days of purification are over,' he said, 'it may be possible, but thy Guru calls. Say thy farewells.'

"Parting tenderly, our ghosts separated. As we, mounting into the regions of clearer vision, moved Westward, I noticed a thread of silvery lustre, stretching far out into the dim distance. To my question:

"'What is this?'

"My companion answered:

"'It is the silver cord, not yet unloosed, which binds us to our bodies.'

"Suddenly a whirring, unintelligible murmur fell upon my hearing.

"To my questioning, my guide made answer:

"'That is the voice of the Viewless races, to whose forms thine eyes are this day closed, by thy teacher's wisdom. Some day, no doubt, thou wilt see them, when more knowledge and experience are thine.'

"Hardly had he finished speaking, when we were caught in a vast cyclone, on whose outer edge we were swiftly whirled away from our direct course.

"'Lay thine hand in mine, and let thy purpose hold fast,' hurriedly whispered my guide. ' When we have passed a semi-circumference, we shall again be drawn on our course, by his will, who watches over us, and already perceives our danger. We are immediately over one of earth's great battles. Thou seest how the fury of thought reaches beyond the physical. Safely and quickly we reached the farther pole and were again moving in the line of direction straight ahead.

"And now, we found ourselves on the brink of a current sweeping irresistibly along, which crossed our way at right angles.

"'This,' said my guide, 'is projected force, bent on its own accomplishment, but it would hurl us into dire straits if caught in it. It has no power, however, on the silver cord of life. We can pass over it.'

"Then rising, rising far beyond all the movement, presently we found ourselves once more in the familiar surroundings. Irresistibly drawn, as when one awakens from a dream, I resumed my natural condition, and the low, sweet tones of my teacher's voice fell upon my ear:

"'Thou hast been much favored,' it said, 'to welcome thy father to the invisible country. I perceived the approaching event, and thus was able to gratify both thee and thy father. It is not necessary that the dead should become visible for mortal converse, but the living also may become visible in distant places, and this is even easier. Thus they may stand on a common plane, until such time as the spirit yields up its astral body, when in company with its soul, it passes on to the condition of rest and assimilation.

"'But you are weary. Retire to thy apartment and to-morrow I will hear thy questions. Take with thee my congratulations for thy prompt obedience, courage and fearlessness, in this new adventure.'

"On the morrow, my Guru said: ' Thou canst understand by the things thou sawest, how dangerous is the astral way to him who adventures without knowledge, or preparation, and yet thou didst see only the ordinary incidents. If to thy sight had been revealed the invisible forms of the hostile races, which crowd all the broad domain called space; if thou couldst have heard their words of discouragement and misleading, perchance even thy high courage might have failed thee.

"'Notwithstanding all this, there have been those, who, being void of wisdom, have hastened to brave these dangers. Is it a wonder, under such circumstances, that the thread of life should be suddenly snapped asunder, and the experimenters themselves precipitated into a hastened doom? It is well, always, to understand the laws and customs of any country into which you contemplate journeying. It may save us some confusion in the end.

"'If thou, hereafter, shalt desire to try thy powers in this direction, look steadily at the coin in thy possession, holding it in the palm of thy right hand. If danger impends, or uncertainty confuses, think of me, as I have taught thee, and the thinking shall be the talisman of safety.'

"With closer and closer attention, and more intense eagerness, I pursued my studies, yet more diligently. I was absorbed entirely in the getting of understanding, for the love of it, regardless of what might be the result or outcome of the possession of that understanding. Nor was I conscious of desire.

CHAPTER IV.

WHILE SITTING, one evening, by myself, the tropical moon shining in all its fervency, and lighting up the whole interior of my apartment, I remembered my Guru's words about the coin. I took it in my right hand. Adjusting my body comfortably in a reclining attitude, I fixed my gaze upon it. Almost instantly, a little thrill passed over me. Then came the feeling of lightness, with which I was already familiar. A moment later, and my astral body was looking at the grosser, bodily vesture, as it lay, immovable and stolid, upon the divan. This was attached to me by a bright cord running from the coin to myself, in some indefinable way, through the body.

"Going down the long flight of steps, I went to the fountain in the garden, and sat down to think. As I mused, the whirring noises, of which I had been so dimly conscious in my first journey, became more and more distinct, until I could hear the converse of the Unseen. Looking up and beyond the limits of the mountain-closed grounds, from which the sounds proceeded, I noticed

70

immediately above the inclosure, a radiant space. No clouds, nor dimness obscured the pellucid eminences along which my clear sight mounted from heighth to heighth, conscious simply of immensity. It was the direct ray from Him of the Seven Builders, who was 'in charge.'

"But beyond the guarded precincts came the sounds to my unveiled ear, which had first attracted my attention. Misty Masses, constantly on the move, shaped themselves to my vision, as ungainly forms, creatures whose horror would overcome the stoutest heart. Monsters, unfinished or half made up, creations of helpless malignance, jostled each other, while out of their malevolent thought, they hurled vain words of terrible import and design at me, so amply protected by the barrier at once transparent and to them impassible, long since firmly set about the temple grounds. We could pass to them, but they could not come to us. Secure, for a few moments I watched the impotent hate of the hostile races, who detest the Good, and all his creatures, and especially man, of whose unbridled, rebellious will, these are the creations. They are a wonderfully prolific cause of misery and suffering to mankind, and one which he little suspects.

"Satisfied with my experiment, I willed to return to my sleeping body. A little constriction, a sense of falling, like the changes of a dream, and I found myself once more in the position of gazing at the coin. This I carefully put away for future use.

"The next morning, my Guru, on meeting me, addressed me at once: ' Thou didst well, my brother, not to adventure farther. The full of the moon is not a favorable season for weak travelers to begin their excursions into the borderlands of the earth.'

"One more month had winged its way. Our studies had brought us to the point, where organized force, unintelligent of itself, could be made to serve man, who was so masterful of himself and his environment as to be able to demand it. The teacher said:

"'In the earlier ages of the world, before man had sworn allegiance to the physical, thereby enslaving his best and highest self, he had dominance over the 'creeping things,' the malformed monsters of immense force. By their strength and enforced labor, were piled up the immortal monuments of antiquity, whose ruins, even, surpass the noblest structures that man has since been able to erect without their help.

"'Do you suppose that our brotherhood, whose Knot here numbers but fifteen in the visible, could have hewn this temple out of the solid rock, to say nothing of the beautifying and adorning and fitting it for its intended purpose, by the labor of our hands only? Not in a million years. When I tell you we have been here only since Atlantis fell, from one of whose provinces we escaped, you will conclude that we have had other help. You have courage and discretion. Come with me!'

"Accompanying him, we descended upon one of the main corridors of the temple. Branching off from the first, at right-angles, toward the heart of the mountain, we entered another corridor inclining downward at an angle of twenty degrees. After walking a long distance, we came at last to a flight of forty-five steps. At the foot of these, passing through a short tunnel, we stood in a waiting or ante-room. Beyond this, through an immense, arched doorway, was, in process of construction, a Hall, whose vastness forced physical man to his relative condition of pigmyhood.

"My Guru told me that it was exactly in the heart of the mountain, and when finished, would be for the convocation of all the brotherhood, throughout the world, and for their instruction in the manifestation of the Unseen, wherever its influence can be perceived in all the spaces of the Infinite.

"It had the shape of an immense sphere flattened at the poles. The solid rock was above, below, all around. In what, to us, would be the path of the ecliptic, was a broad vein of gold, passing entirely around the broadest diameter.

"The virgin gold shone and glittered in the light from nowhere, that made all things visible. There was in sight enough treasure to have bought outright the richest empire upon the earth's surface. Here, it had no value, any more than the other cumbering masses. It served its purpose as an interior decoration, that and nothing more. These wise ones had no need to buy that which was all their own. Did they have occasion for anything from the great storehouse of the unmanifested, theirs was the potency, which could bring it into the visible. The ordinary processes of life faded into nothingness, before the dominance of the Will.

"About two-thirds of the space needed was already hollowed out. Two of the Brotherhood, clad in the usual white robes, stood calmly by, as if overseeing. In their hands they held wands made of some dark flexible material, resembling ebony.

"A word, or signal, passed between them. Moving to the outer circumference, at opposite points, they simultaneously directed their wands forward. At the same instant, a stream of fire, blinding as the lightning's flash, struck the apparently impenetrable rock. Huge fragments as the result, covered the floor with debris.

"Then, out of the farther gloom, two monstrous shapes defined themselves. Seizing the huge blocks, they bore them out of the hall by a tunnel perforated for the purpose. Where has all the rubbish been carried? was the question in my mind.

"'Come and see,' was my Guru's answer to

my unvoiced question. Following the elementals, who were just entering the tunnel with a splinter of rock, tons in weight, we were obliged to walk rapidly to keep them in sight. The passage ended abruptly, at an immense cleft sinking down perpendicularly into the bowels of the earth. Into this, the burden‑ bearers flung the immense mass of rock. Down down, amidst the reverberating echoes, it thundered and roared, for full two minutes, and this was succeeded by a soughing sobbing, deepening by irregular intervals into a long silence.

"'That great rift in the mountain has absorbed the whole of the waste material taken from all the rooms of the temple, save only that used in the building of outside steps, terraces, and colonnades. All the lifting and carrying and carving has been done by the strong, deft agency of elemental force. They do our menial work. This is what they were intended for. Unrestrained they grow mischievous to man's plans, because of the surplus of unemployed strength, but are not malignant.

"'Mankind, in this age, and in the nearest future ages, worshiping blindly a physical idea, will be content only with the making visible to his personal sense of some material form, which is but the outer garb of elemental force. Its rigidity always prevents the full exercise of the power inclosed in the machine of iron, steel and brass. All that he thus accomplishes, might have been obtained in its primitive shape, had he not closed his eyes to all spirit life and power.

"There is but one force, an emanation from the Supreme, which can be seized and apportioned in parcels, by man. These he names according to his own fancies, having no regard for the reality of the thing itself. Potent thought first formulates out of this ever-present plastic material the things called elementals, having no intelligence of their own, but simply potency for accomplishment.'

"'One of our Egyptian Brothers said:

"""The Lord God made man out of the dust of the ground, and breathed into his nostrils the breath of lives." The making out of the dust of the ground, was the formulating of elemental force. The breath of lives is intelligence, the mark set upon man by the Infinite, to distinguish him from other existences, of the same grade of formulation.'

"Returning to the great Hall of Convocation, he continued: 'Our brothers take turns, day by day, at this work. It cannot be pursued uninterruptedly, for we incur the hostility of the unseen races: First, in undertaking so vast a work, which shall still farther extend and strengthen our authority, already obnoxious to them. Secondly, because of their sympathy with those who are forced to serve us. They impede us to the extent of their power. Consequently, we deem it best to have all the advantages possible in our favor. We work in pairs, by turns, resting between, and for the seven days which bring the full moon, on the fourth day, because in the inspiration of its highest rays, all occult powers, for good, develop their highest strength.'

"'Those who travel the other path, seek, on the contrary, the absence of her light. In the old nomenclature, she stood as the symbol of chastity and purity, the favoring patroness of all the good, which born of itself, seeks strength from the same. Then the force sent out by the workers is an exercise of potency which must renew itself. Even the Supreme Intelligence, Itself, at the end of seven days' exercise of the highest potency, is declared to have rested. So do we, in this exercise of our potency.'

"Later on, in my life in the Temple, I was favored with other views of this Hall.

"For my spirit, thirsting constantly for yet more and more instruction, the days flew on. In a conversation about the Astral, my Guru said: 'This is variously called astral light, astral fluid, or simply the astral. It might better be called the astral conditions, for out of it comes everything conceivable, and into it returns and is stored up the essential essence of all things created or creatable. In it is recorded every thought, word or action occurring in the Universe. The Infinite One looks upon it, and sees, even as we look upon our mentality and say: " I remember." The astral then can well be called the Divine Memory. So no essence is lost, no force is lost, no effect of action is lost, but everything is recorded. If we have the key of the recording cipher, and are in alignment with the Truth, no knowledge is impossible for us to obtain. No power that we can handle is beyond our grasp. No wish that we are strong enough to accomplish can be denied us. Failure to receive is simply the consequence of our own weakness. Everything is ours and is fully prepared for us, when we are ready. Ah! how many years of vexatious re-incarnation are necessary to bring us to the acknowledgment of this truth even to ourselves.

"'Whoever will take the pains to train himself can have at his command all the thoughts of the wise and good in all ages. It is best for him always, under all conditions and circumstances, to strengthen his own powers, and not to depend upon the thoughts and deductions of other men, save as starting points for his own reasoning.'

"While he had been talking, I had been transcribing his words for further study, when I should be by myself. Just at this point, I noticed with some little vexation that my ink-horn was empty. He, perceiving my plight, said:

"'Hand it to me.'

"On receiving it, he held it in outstretched hand a single instant, and returned it to me filled to the brim with the finest ink.

"'You see,' he said, 'supplies are everywhere. There is no desert so bare, no wilderness so solitary, but that the supplies necessary for life are close at hand, for those who will, and dare receive.'

"From this time on, to both him and myself, came often supplies for urgent needs out of the astral conditions.

"During the ninth month, my teacher's instructions were more and more pointedly directed towards the utter subjugation of all personal sensation and emotion to the power and direction of the spirit.

"Not only was potency urged for any wish, but all wishes were to be deemed idle and a waste of time, which would not be esteemed worthy of enforcing with all the strength of possible power.

"As my Guru said:

"'Do not formulate any expression of will which has nothing to be gained by its attainment. It is worse than idle, for it divides and scatters force, and success depends always upon the completeness of its focalization. To be thoroughly master of self, one must be able to introvert their personal sense, and instead of receiving impressions from without, receive them from the inner. Instead of dealing with the manifestations of the physical, learn how to gain knowledge through the soul of the astral conditions. This is accomplished by meditation and by the help of introversion, passing into the regions of one's own mentality. He who stands face to face with his own soul, has accomplished very much in his journey toward final attainment.

"'No one can fully describe it. No one can do it for another vicariously. It must be entirely the work of him who is to receive benefit thereby.'

"As the moon rounded into completeness for the tenth time since my preparation commenced, I noticed my Guru frequently looking upon me with an expression of tenderness, for which I could not account. But the mystery was soon solved. On the day of the full moon, as he left me at the usual hour, he said:

"'My brother, tonight one comes to you, to whom you are to listen, but not necessarily to obey. Whatever he may say to you, must be judged by its merits, in the light of your own knowledge. May it be well with thee.'

"At midnight, a slight touch awoke me from a sound sleep. Springing to my feet, I confronted a tall, ashy-gray robed figure, who held in his left hand a crystal globe, that glimmered and sparkled like a big glow-worm. In husky tones, he said:

"'Come with me.'

"Perceiving him to be one of the attendant elementals, I should have refused to comply, if I had not remembered my Guru's parting words.

"So, without question, I followed him. Passing through the brilliantly lighted corridors I was already acquainted with, he turned to the left, into a region in which I was an entire stranger.

The corridors here were so dimly lighted, that the attendant's glow-worm seemed by contrast very bright indeed. Walking rapidly through the various windings, we came at last to a blank wall entirely barring our passage.

"My guide knowing the secret of entrance, for he was the guardian of that department of the temple, put forth the potency of his will within limits. Silently as the grave a door moved back. I followed him into a vast room, whose floor, roof, walls, were one huge deposit of gold, out of which the room had been hollowed. On every hand were great heaps of the yellow metal, and precious stones of every description named upon earth, were piled up, any one of which would have sufficed for a monarch's ransom.

"Waiting a moment or two, until my dazzled senses could comprehend that more than the earth's known wealth was in sight here, the guardian said:

"'I am bidden to tell thee that one-fifteenth of all this treasure is thine. I will transport it for thee, wherever thou seest fit. Thou hast been in the world. Thou knowest what it can bring to thee, of all that man deems most desirable. Beauty, luxury and power are all purchasable, and wealth recreates itself. Thy share is freely offered thee.

"'But thou must also know, if, taking thy portion, thou wilt go into a far country, thou shalt no more return hither, nor again meet the brotherhood in this incarnation, nor perhaps in many others, for its Karma lieth heavy on the shoulders of him who may undertake to bear it. Choose freely, and go thy way if thou wilt.'

"For a single instant, visions of all the elegance, ease, and efficiency such boundless wealth would command among men, flitted before me. Then like the aroma of sweet flowers, that had bloomed long ago, came the memory of my instructor's words:

"'God is All, the Only Real. All else is as unreal as the baseless fabric of a dream.

"My courage and strength came back to me. Rising to my full stature, I ordered my guide to conduct me hence, for this wealth had no value for me, when weighed against the privileges of the Brotherhood. We stepped out of the treasury of the Temple. The door closed behind us with a sullen clang. My guide reconducted me to my own apartment, and suddenly vanished, without taking the trouble to walk away.

"Flinging myself upon my couch, from out the moonbeams came restful quiet, that soon gave me sleep.

"In the morning, on meeting my Guru, a grave smile overspread his face, as he said:

"'And thou hast learned the true value of riches. It is well.'

"Once more, I apply myself vigorously to my daily duties. Week follows week, until another momentous day has come. As we sit at work in the laboratory, a letter drops without warning upon the open scroll before him. He looks at the superscription and breaks the seal. After reading, he hands me the following:

"'Madrid, Spain.

To The Brother-in-charge:

Say to our youngest brother: The heir to the throne of Spain, standing between him and the succession, has passed into the invisible. He is entitled to the Scepter. If he shall so choose, he can be at once transported, hither, and his rights maintained. Let us know his decision at once.

Fraternally,

He Who Watches.'

"'What is your answer?' said my teacher.

"'May I ask you two questions?'

"'Certainly.'

"'Can I, by acceptance, be of any benefit to the Brotherhood?'

"'Not the slightest,' was the answer.

"'Shall I be cut off from the Brotherhood, henceforth?'

"'Most certainly.'

"'Then say to him from me, the next heir is more willing and needy than I, let him receive it.'

"My Guru bowed his head in silent assent. Then taking a sheet of parchment, he wrote thereon, folded and sealed it. Poising it on the end of his stylus, in my full sight, it vanished into thin air. I had unwittingly added another, in the person of the new king, to my list of tormentors; but had, in compensation, advanced one step nearer the perfection of mortal life.

"And now, on the morrow, would commence the twelfth and last month of my probation. My Guru said:

"'Heretofore, you have had help and companionship to sustain you in your trials; but now, for the month to come, you must alone meet your last trial of the novitiate. Tomorrow, at sunrise, you will be conducted to the mount of fasting. For thirty days, save water from the spring, no sustenance must pass your lips.'

"On the morrow, my Guru accompanied me to a little plateau, on the very peak of the mountain, outlooking upon the gardens. Here I found a rock-hewn cell, whose entrance faced the South. Within, a divan, with skins stretched upon it, and a single stone block for a seat, was all the furnishing. Outside the door, a spring clear as crystal, bubbled into, and overflowed a rocky basin.

"Turning to me, my Guru said:

"'You are to sustain your physical self upon that which you have learned. Be faithful. Be strong. Let your thought dwell constantly in contemplation of the Good. Farewell!' I was alone.

"After the first three days, the imperative call of the body for food ceased and the chains which bind together the body and the spirit, loosed their tension. Every morning at sunrise, I drank a few swallows from the spring, then laved my face, hands and feet in the stream issuing from it. Then, going back to my- cell, I gave myself up to communion with the Silence, musing on the infinity and eternity of the One only God.

"Losing my sense of self in this exercise, I would perhaps pass unheeding into the hours of night; or the first beams of the morrow's rising sun would find me still astonished at the immensity of the Soul of the Universe.

"As the days went by, the veil which separates man from the Creator, grew thinner and thinner. The spirit, no longer checked by the importunities and retarding weight of the physical expression, exultantly soared lighter and lighter. Passing the cherubims, and the flaming sword which turns every way, it passed on and on, until the great white throne, symbol of Omnipotence, became continual sight. Time for me ceased to exist. They who, at that time, unknown to me, watched my welfare, say my ecstasy and uplifting increased from day to day.

"On the morning of the twenty-eighth day, I drank from the spring for the last time, and retiring to my couch lay down to meditate. All consciousness of physical weakness or bonds had entirely disappeared. My body showed no sign of weakness. My face was lighted up, as are always the faces of those who are permitted to approach the mount of presence. This is the story of the watchers.

"The experience that came to me was as follows: Shortly after lying down, the impression of freedom and lightness came upon me with the most intense conception.

"It was not the astral separation, but more an assimilation of accretions sublimed and purified concentrating in one mass. The way grew easier and easier, until the light of the Highest burst in full splendor upon my enraptured vision.

"There in the midst of Life and its Principle, enwrapped in the Oneness of All, gazing, gazing with unquenched aspiration for knowledge, at the light, the truth, towards which, in my soul, there was not the least shade of opposition but only the most perfect alignment and harmony, came out of the silence, to my inner sense, the still, small voice, saying:

"'My son, to him that overcometh, will I give the crown of lives.'

"As the sun went down, I came back to the present, and my Guru came also.

"Looking upon me, he said:

"' My brother, thy face tells the story. The light that is not on land nor sea, is upon it. It shines as did the face of one of our brothers in the olden time, who underwent a similar ordeal.'

"Then he put forth his hand, and with the strong grip of the Brotherhood, lifted me to my feet. I was bathed, and sustenance, which man, outside of the Brotherhood, knows not of, was given me for the refreshment of the body.

"Once more, clothed in clean, white, linen robes, I stood in the Hall of Obligation. Kneeling before the invisible occupant of the throne, these words, from our Elder Brother, came to my ears:

"' My younger brother, so far as thou hast been proved, thou hast borne thyself fearlessly and courageously; and thou hast made much progress for thyself into the realms of the unseen.

"' This thou hast done, aided, directed and watched over by our immediate presence, protected from opposing force by the potency of our wills, even as the tender infant is cherished by the arms of its parent.

"' We know that the jewel within is genuine, but no lapidary save thyself can so burnish it as to bring out its greatest beauties, and most valuable qualities. Polish comes not to jewel nor man by lying enwrapped in soft textures, but by attrition against the hardest substances and conditions of the outer life.

"'We have given you the theorems. Are you willing to undertake the demonstration?'

"I bowed assent.

"' You will be conducted from here to your

native land, there to take up the thread of mortal life. To live and act as thou hast been taught in the Light of the Real. Thou shalt seek no fellowship with, nor have any dependence upon the transitory unrealities of time and sense. If at the end of seven years, thy conscience is clear of intent to offend, thou mayst return hither and claim for thyself the degree of the Initiate, and so be able to solve the mysteries of the Second Gate. May Truth and Peace dwell with thee. Remember the obligation of the novitiate.'

"Thus gently dropped the veil of separation, until seven times should roll over my head. Conducted thence, when the morning dawned my Guru came to me.

"'My brother,' he said, ' I would this could be spared thee. But it is the road we all have trod. Attainment comes no other way. If thou hast importunate need of me, in any future time, look upon thy talisman and formulate thy desire, and thou shalt surely and speedily have tidings from me, according to thy necessity.

"' Yet three days dost thou remain with us, for thy bodily rest and refreshment.'

"All too quickly flew the hours in converse and retrospect with my beloved teacher. As the moon rose on the evening of the third day, attendants brought to me the garb of a Spanish cavalier, in which I attired myself. Then through a narrow passage, I was conducted to a wicket in the mountain-side, so cunningly constructed that, from the outside, the most experienced eye would find it difficult to discern.

"Here we paused, and my Guru turning to me said:

"'It is not lawful for me to step beyond the walls, so here we must part. Outside the Temple thou wilt find a horse waiting for thee. Mount him and give him rein and he will bear thee Eastward to the port by the sea, from whence thou didst commence thy journey toward us. There thou canst take ship and go thence to thy ancestral home. Have no thought of curb or rein. Sit easy. He who shall bear thee knows the bidding of the Master. May the night be good to thee. Farewell!'

"Such were his stately words of parting, as tender in their cadence as the caress of a loving mother. The wicket swung wide open. I stepped out and it closed behind me. I was once more outside the walls that had protected me so steadfastly and securely.

"But the Ego that stood there, once again facing the implacable, restless world, was not the impeded, burden-bearing I, who had obtained admittance therein. A new man, like the butterfly from the chrysalis, who had passed from death unto life, the life of the Infinite and Supreme.

"Behind me, the wicket, every vestige of whose existence was lost in the rough face of the precipice. In front of me, a large, splendidly formed, black stallion, every item of whose magnificent form and muscles told truly of superhuman strength. Vaulting into the saddle, I laid the reins lightly upon his neck. Heading north of East, he sprang forward at a speed that seemed to leave the earth beneath him. Hour by hour he moved, his pace showing never a sign of slackening.

"As the light began to grow in the East, he stopped at the country gate of the old fort, where St. Augustine now stands. I dismounted and the huge black without an instant's halt turned on his trail, and was out of sight as suddenly as a flash of lightening.

"With his disappearance, the last link of the chain connecting me with those who had become indissolubly bound to me, seemed to drop away. All the bright hopes in the future manifestations of my existence assumed the dissolving phantasy of a dream. I saw myself a stranger, at the gate of a strange city, moneyless and alone. I sat down on a stone seat outside the wall, with an awful sense of desolation overshadowing me for the first time since, as an invalid, I had been carried into the great temple of ——— Where? Alas! I knew not even its location, and I was banished, perhaps forever.

"In this critical moment, the Master's words sounded in my ear: 'Be of good cheer, thy bur- den will never be beyond thy strength.'

"Half rising, involuntarily I put my hand in

the pocket of my doublet and drew out a purse well filled with the yellow metal, gold, which the Spaniard adores so devoutly. I felt once more comforted, because the Masters had not forgotten the needs of the ordinary life, with which I had again come in contact. I have learned since that they never do.

"But the day came on apace. I could hear the call of the sentry, as the relief passed from post to post. Soon the gates were opened. I requested from the officer of the guard an interview with the commandant, stating I was needy and must have help.

"He stared at me and my accent, but courteously led the way, finishing the grand round, until we reached the castle, where I was conducted into the presence of the chief officer, at his morning coffee. He proved to be one of my comrades in the suite of De Soto. Having escaped the massacre, for especial bravery he had been appointed to his present position.

"He recognized me, and greeted me with the utmost cordiality and friendship, and asked me where I had spent the intervening time.

"I told him I had been nursed and held among the Indians, and finally brought thither.

"'A miracle! A miracle! That these bloody, heathen dogs should ever show grace to a noble, Christian Spaniard. But what dost thou intend to do, Senor?'

"I replied: 'I desire to return to Spain, to see how it fares with my father and my estates.'

"'Thou art in good time, for a Spanish galleon lies in the harbor, whose sails will be spread for favoring breezes on the morrow. Canst thou not wait a month, and bear us company? We shall be honored by thy presence.'

"When I told him my anxiety was pressing, he said:

"'I do not blame thee. Thy impatience is natural. Thou shalt have all the help I can give thee, and may all the saints in the calendar give thee swift journey to thy home.'

"So on the morrow, with such speedy preparation as the shortness of the time permitted, I was again moving Eastward, toward my inevitable destiny.

"How different the return from the coming. Then, the Nemesis of the Past goaded me into constant activity. Now, the intent born of the desire to do good, brought a far different state of feeling. There came to my spirit the possibility of wiping out the stain of blood, by fulfilling the three-fold Rule of Right. So should Karma, the Remorseless, be satisfied.

"Fair winds brought us rapidly to Lisbon. Prom thence I journeyed to my father's house, finding as I already knew, my father dead, and my estate held in waiting by the officers of the crown, as was the custom of the country. I had no difficulty in proving my identity. Then I waited upon the king and queen at the Royal palace, to pay the respects due from the subject.

"My family name gave me audience at once. The queen was very much interested in my recital of the adventures of the ill-fated De Soto. To the request that I detail my adventures with the red men, I answered but little, speaking mostly of my wounded condition, the care bestowed upon me, and my life amongst them. Description of the temple, or anything pertaining thereto was too sacred to be imparted to another who had neither sympathy nor perception to understand, even if it had been lawful for me to tell.

"The audience was finally over, and permission was granted me to -withdraw to my estate. There I fitted up a laboratory, modeled upon the one in which so much pure, unalloyed happiness had come to me, during the past year.

"Here for another year, I lived contentedly, pursuing my studies and recovering from the fatigue of my journey. To this was added the care of overseeing my estate and dependants. At the end of the year, a message by special courier from the king, informed me:

"'It was' a great deprivation to his majesty that I was not seen at court.' This courteously worded document, of course, was a most emphatic order.

"Regretfully, I made my preparations, and soon found myself in daily attendance at one of the most brilliant courts of that period in Europe. Indeed, it has rarely been equalled in the world for its wealth, beauty and learning.

"Appointed to an office in the household, a bachelor, rich, and of fair presence, could there be wanting anything to make me happy? To me, all this seemed rust, dust and mold. There was no satisfaction whatever in any of it. But I, at the first, submitted, because it had been the Master's will and teaching, that obedience to the symbol of law, wherever met with, was necessary, because it led to obedience to the law itself, which is man's first duty. All true law is of the Good—is the Good.

"Having no ambitions to satisfy, no schemes which set myself and my interests over and beyond the interests and selfishness of others, I had many friends, or rather those who called themselves friends. But I must confess I was startled, and at the first deeply pained, as my intuitive perception revealed their motives. Then the motive entirely overshadowed the apparent action, bringing to me in all its force, a perception of the weakness of dependence upon smiles or honeyed words. In spite of all this, I was popular, and a favorite with the king, to whose business intrusted to my charge, I gave my best attention, because it was the duty I owed him.

"One day, when in attendance upon his majesty, without any previous preface he said:

"'Senor, why do you not marry? Are there no

ladies in all our realm fair enough for thee, or didst thou leave a fairer inamorata in that savage Western country?'

"'Nay, your majesty,' I replied. ' I am heart-free, because the sex have no charms for me, nor I for them.'

"'But, Senor, I have no liking that through caprice my oldest families should become extinct. It were well that you select a wife, and thus add to the dignity and peace of the kingdom.'

"I simply bowed, and the matter was dropped. Not many days after this, I received orders to be present at a reception in the palace. Here I was presented to the younger daughter of one of the most noble houses of the kingdom. She was a most fitting consort for me, in every respect, as to family, station or wealth. In addition to this, she was most ravishingly beautiful. I was given to understand that it was the king's pleasure, that I should seek the hand of this beautiful and desirable maiden in marriage. If I did not concur, without good excuse, his anger might be turned against me.

CHAPTER V.

WITHOUT DELAY, seeking audience of the king, I begged leave of absence, on plea of urgent business, for a week, to visit my estates. It was graciously granted. In haste, on horseback, with only a single attendant, I rode back to the only spot on the whole broad earth, which now seemed to link me to a past, whose claims upon me were ineffaceable, no matter what might be my condition or actions. Retiring to my laboratory, with orders that I should not be disturbed, I threw myself upon my divan. The struggle between the physical and the spiritual commenced.

"Clearly, without the dimming of a tone, or the slighting of a detail, came before me the advantages of the connection. Over this delineation, the purely sensual did not fail to cast its lurid light. In contrast, was also presented the greater pleasure and purer joy, which gives the only happiness of this world. I fully perceived how much of satisfaction to the spirit lay in the consciousness of attainment, in the enlarging of the soul's powers, and its area of influence. I could not forget that which was promised me, and already within my reach. I could not barter off my spiritual birthright, for a mess of physical pottage.

"In my agony of indecision, my robe, which I always wore in my laboratory, had become disarranged at the neck. As I reached this last conclusion, my hand came in contact with the jewel that still hung about my neck. A thrill passed over me, followed by a sense of calmness and peace.

"I saw a man and woman standing together, he pledging to her, by an irrevocable oath, his soul's devotion. As these recurring memories floated out of the unseen, Into my consciousness, my inner sense heard a calm, far-off voice which had so often been to me the sweetest melody. It said:

"'My brother! She to whom you are pledged waits thee. To accept or reject, is not thy greatest trial. If thou canst take her with the mutual understanding of unviolated chastity, in all time to come, it is well. Thou shalt soon enough, in the future, know of that which still remains. This is of thy Karma. Words and oaths do not vanish as lightly as they are spoken, but go forth to the accomplishment of that where unto they are sent through all the ages.'

"The voice ceased. Little by little dawned upon my understanding, the trial now opening before me.

"She who was to be my bride, was beautiful beyond comparison. All her outward physical attractions had been kissed into full maturity, in all the lusty vigor of youth, by the fervid sun of the tropics. Unless the spirit controlled, the fire within might not only consume itself, but also all with whom it came in contact. When she should be mine under the law, owned in body by me, as completely as the beast is owned, who has no redress, obedience to the slightest caprice of my will her man-made law, what then? The unknown quantity was her own desire. The appeal to the lower consciousness of the physical, the blind, brutal instinct was as complete as concurring circumstances could make it.

"Should I, as a human being, with the tidal waves of Karmic conditions barely held in check, be able to live constantly in such an atmosphere, with such surroundings, and successfully resist the seething torrents of emotion? One could flee from temptation, and thus break its power, but to dwell in it constantly; to steel one's powers, voluntary and involuntary, against it hour by hour, ever on the watch for the first fanning of the tiniest flame, by act, word or deed—did mortal ever accomplish such labor? It has been so said. Suppose, in some unguarded moment should come the rush of the ever watchful, never satisfied and keenly intense physical. If that physical, seeking ever through spiritual perception to enhance its own enjoyment, should bear away by its impetuosity all oaths, all teaching, and all knowledge, what then?

"For reply, came the sound of words, vibrating out of past ages, binding irrevocably her soul to mine in all cycles yet to come. Out of this, had come to me my present knowledge of this trial, and I must submit. Would she know? Would she care?

"The event was fixed beyond my power of choice. The acceptance, the struggle, the victory! Ah! would I be so fortunate? All lay in the misty realms of the unrolling. It been decreed in the past, by myself, as a Karmic condition.

"Summoning an attendant, I found that it was the third day since I had entered my inner room. So bathing, and changing my apparel I spent the rest of the week in the affairs of my estate.

"Returning to court, I announced to the king my desire to propose for the lady's hand. She was an orphan and the king's ward. In due time the lady signified her acceptance of my suit, and our betrothal took place. This was followed by the marriage ceremonies under the direction of the Holy Catholic Church, celebrated with all the pomp and magnificence becoming the families of two of the peers of the realm, both related to the crown.

"As, over clasped hands, the vows of mutual allegiance were spoken, a full-blown oleander blossom formed between our hands, and a single word, 'Isa,' sounded clearly and distinctly above all the rush of the surrounding ceremony. It thrilled all my pulses with indescribable joy. I glanced at my wife. A smile of recognition and content parted her lips, as her eye flashed one look at me. A recurring memory of being what I was not then, of the token of a pledge, which had now reached fulfillment, presented itself to my mind. When I came to myself the ceremony was finished. With the oleander blossom carefully preserved, by easy stages we made our journey to my ancestral home.

"The suite of rooms occupied by us were those formerly belonging to my parents, and the scene of the memorable ' visit out of the body,' on the occasion of my father's death. They were in a wing of the chateau, and faced East, West, and South. They looked out upon the foot-hills of the Sierra de Guadarama, and upon the soft-flowing of one of the minor branches of the Tagus.

"My steward, a member of a family whose sons and sons' sons had served ours as faithfully and loyally as we had served the king, maintained the whole domain in a high degree of cultivation. Vineyards and orchards of pomegranates and figs extended away, even to the bare acclivities of the mountains.

"The rooms were arranged as a common chamber, with two sleeping apartments and their accompanying dressing-rooms opening out of it. These, in compliance with my orders, had been renovated and refurnished for the occasion, thinking more of her pleasure than mine.

"When, as the twilight approached we met in the retiring room, and for the first time found ourselves alone together, I was charmed with her manners and gentleness. We sat side by side on a divan, and as we rested and chatted it seemed as if we had always known each other. Little by little it dawned upon me, from something she said, that my wife also possessed occult knowledge. Finally turning to her, I asked a question which can be answered in set phrase only by a person 'who hath wisdom.' Readily, and evidently with a full comprehension of all I sought to know, and glad, with a great joy, thus to give me the assurance I desired, the correct answer came.

"I was so overwhelmed with this realization of hopes, which I had, apparently, no basis for cherishing, I could make no reply.

"After a few moment's silence, she continued: "'My husband, I have been conscious of your struggle and its outcome. Until you had made your decision, I had no power to interfere, either to assist or retard. But now I may tell you. I, also, am a novitiate, seeking knowledge, and as two are stronger than one, together we may tread the path, and hope for accomplishment. I know, as you know, that they who dwell within the power of the

Spirit have no sex. But that which we both seek can be reached in its highest only by unstained loyalty to one another, a friendship of which the lust- stained, material world has no conception.'

"'*Carissima mia!*' my thoughts came at last in a torrent of impetuous words: 'Your avowal makes me happy beyond conception. Work that is shared by pure friendship, and a common interest, will bring far more than doubled result. We, acting in unity, complements of each other, having eliminated the disturbing elements of the lower planes, may reasonably expect far more development than we could possibly look for if struggling alone for that which we both desire, and are both seeking. May the Beloved Masters guide us, and may both be willing to be guided!'

"A feeling of peace, of blessing, of rest, beyond conception, as if all the harassing influences of physical condition were quieted forever, enveloped me completely. From the expression on my wife's face, I saw that she, too, was in the same current of benediction.

"The worries and bewilderments of life are the result of man's weak thoughts, selfish desires and cross-purposes, poured into the thought- currents of the Universe, which, like the emptying of sewers into a clear, mountain stream, contaminate and utterly defile the whole. In the radiance of the pure current of thought, which I recognized as flowing direct from the Brotherhood so dear to me, I looked at my wife and loved her as a man might love an angel.

"Thus in silence and content we sat. In a little niche over the high-arched south window, a low-burning lamp, filled with perfumed oil, gave out a delicious fragrance, while below it, in the untapestried space, a great stream of silvery light, from the full moon, flooded the room.

"Unspeakably restful, I grew passive, and in the moonlight a vision shaped itself. A stately palace, standing in gardens of richest bloom, fanned by perfume-laden breezes. Within this, I see a man and a woman. As they come distinctly to my perception, I hear words, which once uttered can never be recalled, but are sealed up, a law unto the soul for generations, in the ages to come. The scene fades into the outer presence; my eye falls upon the oleander blossom, given me out of the Silence, on the altar steps, which now stood in a little antique vase of water. It had, thus far, retained its freshness and beauty. As I looked at it, it moved with a shivering thrill. A sighing moan shaped itself into the words:

"'The pledge is reclaimed.'

"A little heap of fine dust, scattered over the water, the vase and the table on which it stood, was all that remained of the token of four thousand years.

"As memory recurred to past-incarnations, I seemed to remember, as one recalls a far-off boyhood, a point in eternity, that I recognized as a duration of previous life. I then understood more clearly than ever, how the law of Karma crystallized, by the voluntary consent of my own will and the force of spoken thought, had again brought us together, not to revel in tropical effeminacy, the slaves of physical desire, but far beyond, on the rising spirals of race progress. Turning to my wife, with a single touch of lip to forehead, I say gently:

"'Isa, dear, I am rejoiced beyond measure to know you again.'

"'My lord remembers,' she replied in her soft-flowing, Castilian speech, ' He who keeps faith loyally and wittingly, is mightier than the founder of cities, and shall receive just recompense.'

"From that hour, all difference of sex seemed to have passed away. I loved my Isa, as a father a son, or as one brother another, with a fervor born of reality, as the angels love In the unseen, we are told that all the accidents of the physical fade away. But love, the inspiring element of the Divine nature, does not fade, nor cease to be; but purified of the rush and whirl; of the tingling blood; the panting breath; and the quickened heart-beats, this mighty force of tenderness, the only worthy motive for self-abnegation, lives forever. As the angels in heaven are neither married, nor given in marriage; so we two dwelt together, as might two friends of the same sex, loving each other with a most tender and devoted love.

"Day by day we pursued our studies, continually interested in each other's progress, and anxious for the utmost possible attainment. It was true also, that a much greater gain was possible from the operating of two as one, than from the efforts of the single individual; a quicker perception, a more intense persistence, and a larger potency, when required. I rejoiced in her accomplishments and perfection; in her wisdom and friendship. Thus another year went by, and it became necessary for us to return to court for a season, to pay our respects to our sovereign, and then we should be at liberty, if we desired, to reside on our estate.

"It was the evening before our journey. We were sitting as at the first evening at home, in our common chamber, the whole interior flooded with the light of the full moon. We had been discussing the spirit's potency, and how far it might be able to reach into the future, and thus become certain knowledge. As our thoughts became more and more intense we had lapsed into silence. Suddenly, came the voice of the old-time Isa:

"'My lord would like to see that which comes. Take the jewel thou wearest, in thy right hand. Place thy left hand in my right and look.'

"I did as she directed.

"A faint odor of the lotus diffused itself about me, growing stronger and stronger. The moonlight became more and more substantial, until, as when one looks over a broad landscape under a clear light, I saw an accident, fatal but for interposing arms, a temptation and a terrible struggle, of which more bye-and-bye in its place. The end was not revealed to me, being cut off by the perturbation of my mental conditions. The disturbed harmony brought me again to full consciousness and an inner perception of Isa's words, recalled afterwards under far different circumstances:

"'Oh, my lord! That which is to be must be. Be master of thyself and all will be well.'

"A lovely day, even for sunny Spain, smiled upon our cavalcade next day as I looked back from the last point of view, upon the place so full of happy memories, unalloyed by a single cruel remembrance. Surely the world was not so bad a place as poet and painter had pictured it.

"I pass over the commonplace incidents of our journey and our cordial reception at court by both the king and queen, who had both conceived a great liking for us. We located our establishment, conforming so far to the unwritten laws as not to excite remark, and yet so arranging that our time should not be all consumed by the social Juggernaut, but might leave us some space to sow, in the quiet, astral fields, the seed for thoughts which would bring to us as we might desire.

"It was our rule to meet all demands that were legitimate, but not to seek the inner circle of the whirl of gayety. After a few months the outside pressure lessened. We acquired a reputation for sedateness which served us well in protecting us from unreasonable demands from those who have no appreciation of the pearls of greatest price.

"The king, however, would not hear of my retirement from public life. So the hope of return to the privacy of my own domain was thereby frustrated, much to my annoyance. So two years went by. At the end of that time as we sat together in the Silence, according to our daily custom, my wife said:

"'My lord, I am summoned to meet my Guru. I shall be gone three months. I hope it will be well with us both when we meet again.'

"It was the season when the court was resting from its round of excitement, and she would not, therefore, be missed nor specially inquired for during so short an absence.

"I missed her sorely. Without the childish feeling of irreparable loss, there was still the sensation of a lack in the power to attain my utmost potency, and a need of incentive to its use. Never until now, had I realized how large an integral part of myself my wife had become. It was a withdrawal of intent of potency, rather than of ability to act. It was a feeling of incompleteness, of being only part of myself. I found these feelings coming to me most strongly at the hours we were wont to spend together.

"As a consequence, I sought diversion by active,

physical exercise, horseback riding and such other means of similar nature as were close at hand. She had been absent two months when, restless and disturbed by the feeling of dissatisfaction in the accomplishment of my labors, I mounted my Arabian, and, as the shadows lengthened in the closing day, started for a ride.

"Giving rein to my horse, I rode without thought as to whither my course lay, being intent only on the fact that I was riding. Reaching the outskirts of the suburbs, I still rode on for three or four miles, in that dazed condition in which one feels himself desirous of solving some important problem and yet, for inexplicable reasons, unable to grasp the key of the position.

"At last the restlessness of my horse brought me back to my normal condition. I perceived a rapidly rising cloud that betokened a coming gust of wind and rain, if not worse. Turning homeward, the moan of the rising wind and the first scattering patter of the raindrops warned me to hasten.

"Putting my horse to a gallop, I had reached a little knoll bordered by large trees when there came a blinding flash, a roar and rush, as an immense cedar of Lebanon fell just opposite. In its falling the sweeping limbs dragged me from my rearing horse and left me insensible upon the earth, while my horse, riderless, made the best of his way home.

"The chateau on the estate, where I had

fallen, was but a short distance from the scene of the accident. It belonged to a young and beautiful widow whose husband, a wealthy and disagreeable old Don, had died soon after my return from the West.

"The fall of the tree by the bolt, and the galloping of a riderless horse, were noticed by some of the serving men. They came out as soon as the storm ceased, with torches, to investigate. Finding me still insensible and wet, they carried me on an improvised litter into the chateau. The majordomo had been in attendance upon the lady at court and knew me. He announced my unceremonious arrival to the widow.

"She ordered the best attendance in the house to be given me, and messengers were dispatched in hot haste for a physician.

"I was tenderly disrobed and put to bed in the room of the former master of the chateau. As I slowly came to my senses the surgeon arrived.

"He examined me carefully and found that although no bones were broken, I had a severe contusion on the back of my head, which would doubtless have killed me if my fall had not in some mysterious manner been broken. My right limb also was severely wrenched, in being pulled violently from the stirrup. The shock and the wetting promised a fever. I felt as if I were a mass of aching heat.

"When the doctor had finished his examination

he sat a few moments in silence. Then, as he rose to go, fixing his piercing but kindly eyes upon mine and laying a hand, delightfully cool and soft, upon my forehead, he said:

"'My son, I will send you a potion. But you may sleep.'

"After directions to the attendants, he left me, promising to call on the morrow.

"The intense pain in my head and limbs seemed to leave me at once. When the messenger returned with the potion, to all appearances I was sound asleep. But the fact really was this: My astral body had heard a far-distant voice, and by permission (as in cases of delirium) had lifted itself beyond the consciousness of pain, resting quietly just above the unconscious body. As one, reclining upon the bank of a clear pool, studies its contents, so I, the real Ego, was obeying the direct' of that far-off voice:

"'Look carefully and remember for future use.'

"As I looked, I saw that the difference in the ultimate atoms, was, first, those which were alive or nourishing were capable of showing magnetic polarity at different tensions. The dead atoms had no such power. This was the difference between death and life. Manifested vitality was the result of susceptibility to electrical action. There was in the varying substance of the several organs, a difference in the power of tension, which changed the order of union, so that each following its own law of structure, remained, as at the beginning, adapted to its own work. The liver was always hepatic in its substance; the lungs always parenchymous. The laws of polarity and tension governed all. I saw also that the rapid and varying changes of polarity caused all the phenomena of mental action and nerve force. The slight movement discernible in this changing condition gave a false idea of vibration, which was not a change of place, but a change of condition. This view made perfectly plain to me how thought acts in manifestation. I could see how a certain uniform change of polarity and tension would be regarded as a standard. If it went above this, *sthenic* diseases, or inflammations and fevers, would be the result. If they fell below, then the *asthenic* diseases of dissolution, inertness in manifestation, and death, would be the consequence.

"As I watched my servant the body, I could see the forces adjusting themselves to the normal *status* impressed thereto by the influence of a strong will potentially projected from an entity near at hand, aided and directed by another more powerful will, afar off. These acted, first upon my own will, thence, through that, seizing upon my mentality, the force was transmitted to the physical throughout all its atoms. This proved to me, that all physical change is under control of the directing spirit of each line of organization, and all subject to the immutable law of creative thought.

"No one can injure, by occult means, the body of another, except through the soul force, to which that body belongs, and even to do this, the spirit must consent to its own dishonor. The potency of a strong will acting out of the silence, may move the spirit strongly, even against its own desires, for a little space. In that case, the person would be psychologized, or the unwilling consent of the spirit might for a little time be so misused, as to permit even a debasement of the body.

"Along with the formulation of these conclusions in my mentality, a deep and harmonious peace began to envelop my whole being. Sleep, the unconsciousness that presages rest and healing, wrapped me in its blessed folds.

"When consciousness again came to me in awakening, pain and soreness had left my body, but strength, which can only be the result of action in sequence, was still lacking.

"The morn of a day, such as can be known only in Spain, brought my attendants. I was able to rise and dress, and be removed to a *salon* adjoining my sleeping apartment. Here I was visited by the surgeon, who announced his gratification at my rapid recovery, but evinced no surprise. He sat chatting with me a few minutes, and looking me full in the eye, he dropped, as if incidentally, two words. A flash of recognition passed from eye to eye.

"'I know of thee, my brother,' he said, 'for I too am a student and seeker. Obligations not to be put aside, will prevent my advancement and attainment, as will be your privilege and right. So far, however, as I am permitted, I walk side by side with you. Always, no matter what may be our present relative positions, you can depend on my supporting sympathy. I shall rejoice when you are glad, and sorrow when you weep.

"'You have one more true friend in Spain.'

"Thus speaking, he arose to go, and placed his right hand on my forehead. It was a small, shapely, pleasant hand. On the little finger was an antique ring, holding a sapphire of most intense color. The effect of the soft touch was most marvelous. An accession of strength seemed to flow naturally through my veins. It was not an evanescent sensation, as when one takes a stimulating draught, but rather the strength of perfected healing. In wishing me good morning, he said his services were no longer necessary.

"After he had left me, I sat quietly in the reclining position in which my attendants had placed me. Directly before me was an open doorway, and a broad verandah. Through this the delicious breath of the morning brought inspiring vigor. In full view, beyond, lay the winding river, and plains, and vineyards of fair Spain.

"Looking upon all this, I floated along on a

great current of content.

"Without warning, there came a little shock. An unexplainable feeling of unrest and disquiet touched me. Nothing in the relative bearing of the visible had changed, it could not come from the outer. As this faint ripple in the harmonious flow of the thought current forced itself upon my notice, a servant entered, bearing a little perfumed note from the hostess.

"'Would it be the Senor's convenience, to permit the Senora to wait upon him in person, and congratulate him upon the fortunate outcome of his terrible accident?' So ran the lines of the dainty, brief message.

"Of course, I consented, eagerly perhaps, my mood seeking relief. But as I held the note in my hand, I had occasion afterward to remember, that the emanations from it were pungent and sharp. To my inner vision came plainly a view of the temple in the mountains of the faroff West. I heard once more the grave, tender words of our Elder Brother: 'We have given you the theorems, are you willing to undertake the demonstration?' What did it all mean? It was not long before I knew.

"A scarcely perceptible, soundless movement, and through the hangings of an inner door, a little to my left, in plain view to my half- dreamy vision, came the Senora and her duenna.

"A subtle fragrance floated about and preceded

her, captivating the senses even before the whole exquisite picture was perceived. The archway was heavily curtained with crimson hangings from Damascus. Her tiny, slippered feet, just peeping from her draperies, were nestled in an African tiger's skin, spread before the doorway. As the curtain dropped, she stood squarely, a most winsome figure, a little above the medium height. Her form, perfect in proportions, and most exquisitely rounded, was set off enchantingly by the half-concealment of her white, gauzy apparelling. Her hair and eyes black as the gathered intensity of a tornado; her lips red as the sea-washed coral; and her small, exquisitely-formed hands, all told of the cultured sequence in family descent. On her cheeks, the dusky blaze, never quite extinct, betrayed the hot blood of the tropics, roused, as when it sees that which it desires to possess, within its reach.

"Her magnetic beauty was the first overwhelming impression. It was worthy of imperial palaces. Behind this, a lurid fire surged, in thought, through my long-repressed nature, then a blank. It was like the prairie fires, consuming, with their long, red tongues, at one swoop, the dry, rank herbage, leaving behind only blackened refuse.

"It was a life-time in an instant. Recovering myself, I heard her gracious words in the softest Gastilian, as she said:

"'Is the Senor recovering from his accident?'

"'Thanks, Senora, one could hardly refrain from recovering rapidly, when attended by so much kindness and beauty. Please be seated.'

"At a sign from her mistress the duenna drew up a low, cushioned seat to my side, which my hostess occupied herself, while her companion discreetly betook herself out upon the verandah, and waited for farther orders.

"Here, seated where her flashing eyes could look into my own, she beguiled my loneliness. She made me tell her of my adventures while with De Soto, meantime filling my whole organism with her peerless and ripened magnetism, until the bonds of ascetic training loosened somewhat, and faint flushes called my attention to the fact that the law of sequence had again builded walls of clay out of warm Southern blood. The first impulse was: Never mind this once, let me float on the current, and enjoy as other men enjoy. Then came the memory of the words of obligation, spoken before witnesses, in that far-off Hall, and also of my companion, friend and helper, my wife.

"Still, the witchery of the perfect physical beside me increased in its intensity. The sudden rebellion of my own lower self grew more arrogant and assertive. Cool enough, as yet, to be master of the situation, I called to my relief the forces who were bound to help in any emergency, and thus maintained my composure. I made no outer sign, but the mental effort of will power brought into my face a strained expression. The lady's quick eye noticed this.

"'Ah, Senor! But I am tiring you. You have made me very happy until I forgot you were an invalid. Your descriptions are so charming. May I see you again to-morrow?'

"'Senora, it will be a pleasure,' I replied. Calling her duenna, she vanished like a dream, and I was again alone with myself.

"Strange as it may seem, the strength flowing from her had brought healthful energy and physical healing. I felt better in body for the interview. But, as I reviewed the situation, I was far less self-confident than I might have been under contrary circumstances.

"It is needless to recall in detail the incidents of that week of rest from labor, nor of the Senora's daily visits, nor of the shaping of her purpose to bring me to respond to her partiality becoming every day more and more openly expressed. But the end of all human conditions comes sooner or later. On the morrow I was to return to the city as well and strong as ever.

"I have said that my apartments were those of the old Don. I had retired early, sleeping soundly for the first three hours, when I awoke with a start and that full sense of wide-awakeness which is the result of astral warning. My face was so turned that the partition separating the Senora's apartments was in full view, and plainly visible by the light from the shaded lamp left burning through the night. Just opposite me was a full length portrait of herself, by one of the most celebrated artists of the time.

"As I lay looking at it, it seemed to move. I rubbed my eyes and looked again. Noiselessly as the shifting of the curtain of night, it had moved up, leaving the frame undisturbed. Just within it, clad in her elegant *robes de nuit,* fresh and charming as Venus rising from the sea, stood the original of the portrait. With a smile, in which desire, tenderness and anxiety were blended, she advanced to my bedside, and seated herself thereon.

"It was a moment of moments. An ascetic of years' standing faces his conquered lower self, roused into active revolt by the last few days of companionship with this woman, as it had not been since in ungovernable rage he had stained his hands in the blood of a fellow creature.

"On the other hand, this widow, fair beyond compare, would hear nothing but the accomplishment of her own caprice ; could understand nothing but the satisfying of her own desires. Mature, elegant, refined, even in the height of her passion, appealing to me first with caresses and finally in tears. My refusal was not born of unsustained mortal strength, but of the firmness of purpose gained in the mountains, and the help of the Brotherhood. With eyes suffused with tears, at last she said:

"'Senor, I have offered you all that a woman can give. Am I, indeed, so repellent to you, that you must refuse? I am entirely at your mercy. I hope, at the least, you will keep my secret.'

"'Senora,' I replied, ' if you knew how bitterly I should wound and offend by doing this thing, my consent would turn your love to contempt. I am a Spanish gentleman. A gentleman always keeps a lady's secrets.'

"She turned and left me, never once looking back. The portrait slid noiselessly back to its place. It was done. I was alone. I lay quietly. The passion that had boiled within me changed to a pitying tenderness for her who had become for all the rest of her present life my bitterest enemy.

"The Senora, under the plea of sudden illness, did not appear, on the morrow, to bid me farewell when I made my departure, but all was courtesy and politeness as I rode forth to my own home, with my attendants.

"Arriving at my palace, my attention was engrossed with many things. In my hours of meditation, I did not feel that I had aught to congratulate myself for, except the very narrow margin of escape. I felt humbled to think I had not risen so far above all temptation, as to be able to put it entirely aside, without the consenting thereto and insurrection of the whole physical self.

"The days wore by, and my wife returned. When we were alone together, she remarked:

"'My lord, your trial must needs come. It is nothing you willingly sought nor desired. I feel honored, that in all the conflict there was no thought of faithlessness in your promise to me, nor any yielding of the real, higher self to the onward rush of all physical life. You are not to feel condemned because the animal tugs at the leash. That is a part of the manifestation of the law of vitality. It was held within bounds by the unaided desire of your own spirit, which thus attracted to yourself the forces needed for such accomplishment. You have come out conqueror. Be wise and circumspect, and all shall be well.'

"For the next few years my time went rapidly and uneventfully. Three months before the expiration of the seven years from the day I left the great temple, I was sitting in my private apartment alone, with bolted doors.

"Rousing from a reverie, into which I had fallen, I looked up, and there standing in my presence as when I last saw him, was my Guru. Rising, overcome with a transport of joy, I flung myself at his feet.

"'Arise, my brother,' said the far-off, well-known voice. ' As thou earnest once, so have I now come hither. I bring thee tidings. Within ten days, the king will delegate to thee a difficult and delicate mission, which shall bring thee to us. The mission is prompted by those who hate thee, but it is for thy good. Make no pause, but hasten to obey the mandate of thy sovereign. Thy wife will safely await thee here. Make thy preparations, take thy instructions, and sail at once for the port from which thou earnest.

"'On the night after thy arrival, go to the spot where seven years ago thou didst leave thy horse and thou shalt find him waiting for thee. Mount, and give him rein.

"'The king's business shall have attention. But thou needst not give thy mind to it, nor be uneasy about it, for it will be in safe hands. The Brotherhood have called thee on thy obligation. Come!'

"Happy beyond measure, I looked up to thank him, but he had gone.

"On the third day thereafter, I was bidden to an audience with the king. After some consultation on various trivial matters, he said:

"'Senor, you know something of our dominions in the "New World."' I bowed assent. 'We need a trusty messenger to our cousin, who has charge of our Southern Empire. We know your loyalty and bravery. Will you undertake it for us?'

"'My lord, the king,' I replied,' It has been a proud memory of our family, that to hear the king's voice was to desire the king's wish. I, certainly, shall not be first to change the reading.'

"'It is well said, Senor. You will make your

preparations at once. One of the royal galleons, in commission lies in harbor, waiting for thee. Your instructions will be handed you sealed, to be opened when you are ten days at sea. The galleon, also, sails under orders. A prosperous voyage, Senor.' And the audience was ended.

"Had I been in any way dependent upon the king's good will, I should most certainly have been disturbed by the undercurrent of the inter-' view, for I perceived that my enemy, the widow, had so far influenced the king, as to compel him to believe that, owing to my relationship to the throne, I was a dangerous rival, and rivals are less harmful when banished than when present. As no pretext could be devised for open disgrace, it was deemed best that diplomatically I was to be buried in the savagery of the New World.

"My ready acquiescence surprised the king, whose heart misgave him, with the feeling that he had over-reached himself. Also, the sealed instructions were revealed to me, which were to seek Mexico, and there, as special envoy, to strengthen the Spanish cause, which, I could perceive, was fast waning, founded, as it was, upon cruelty and blood.

"But all this was nothing to me, for my orders were from those of whom the king, sitting on the throne, was but the puppet; and with all my old-time energy, I prepared to obey them.

"Bidding my affectionate wife good-bye, with

the earnest wish that the thoughts from her should be for the strength and will to obey and accomplish, I found myself on the Spanish ship^ with all sails set, moving toward the place of all places where I most desired to be.

CHAPTER VI.

WHEN OPENED, my instructions left to my charge, under ordinary circumstances, the execution of certain impossible conditions. The attempt at accomplishment would probably bring death, and the failure to attempt, disgrace. The trap was skillfully laid. Many a just and good man has, in the history of the world, gone forward bravely to his end in a similar manner.

"The instructions, to the Commander of the ship, were to land me, and return at once, without regard to my wishes, or any method of my coming back. The design was that which sends forth an exile, without the expectation of return. Had I been engaged in any other business than that of the Brotherhood, I might have been at the least uneasy at the unfriendly look of the scheme, so evidently working against me, but I felt that all else was as naught, if so be I might look into the faces of those so loved and revered by me.

"The winds were favorable, the weather all that could be desired. The good ship seemed to be drawn as if by a huge magnet, on its way, so swift and steady was its course. This was so continuous in its action that it became a subject of remark amongst the crew. Passengers there were none, save myself. The voyage was made solely for my benefit.

"At last, the shores of the New World were again visible, and the officers of the ship congratulated me on my short and prosperous journey. I was heartily welcomed by the commandant of the fort. I told him I had special business for the king, in the interior, and asked the usual permission to be absent three months, if necessary. It was willingly accorded.

"As the twilight deepened, I passed beyond the outer line of sentinels. Where, seven years before, my horse had left me, out of the gathering gloom appeared waiting for me the animal who had brought me hither. Naught was changed about him, only he seemed to gladly recognize me, a feeling I returned in full measure.

"Without hesitation I sprang into the saddle, and yielded to the horse's guidance. Swiftly and easily I was borne along. His long stride was like the waving of huge wings. In the darkness, I could distinguish nothing but the swift, onward movement, hour by hour. As the dawn grew wide, I could see in the gray distance the turrets and peaks of the mountain temple. When the first beam of the rising sun rested on the cliff where my days of fasting, preceding the final trial, were passed, my steed stopped at the face of the precipice, and I dismounted. As I did so, the gate opened, and passing within the charmed boundary, I was received by my Guru.

"'Welcome, my brother! Obedience and promptness are jewels which command the wearer to favorable notice from his Master. Thou art to rest four months, undergo four months' preparation, when thou wilt receive the degree of the neophyte, then another four months' rest, and again thou wilt return to take up the world's burden, and prove thyself worthy to advance still another degree. Thou knowest the way to thy former resting place. The Chamber of Peace is ready for thee.'

"He laid his hand upon my head; a feeling of peace, wiping out all worries and anxieties of every sort, either for the past or present, or the future, enveloped me like a garment. All emotion merged into one sensation, that of restfulness. As I mounted the well-remembered steps to the chamber looking to the East, the outside world, which is so much to most men, became of small consequence, beside the conviction that within myself was all, and that I was responsible for all, to myself. This relieved me of the last traces of the world's burden.

"Having bathed, changed my apparel and received refreshment, the day passed in quiet unutterable. The rest of the Infinite, of Nirvana, was mine. I passed day after day in conversation with the Brothers; in questionings of matters that had perplexed, but which here cast no shadow; and in contemplation of all the Infinite power and goodness.

"The allotment of rest passed quickly, and the beginning of the preparation was close at hand. It was the evening before the first day, and as in former times, an almost full moon flooded the white, marble chamber with its glorious brightness. Suddenly, apparently gliding along out of the moonbeams, came into my presence an Ancient One. Standing beside me he said: "Son of my brother, look up, and tell me what thou beholdest.' I obeyed, and as I looked, that which to personal sense is invisible, the air, became surcharged with life and manifestation. The atoms appeared, increased, diminished and disappeared, while through all, over all and permeating all, was the brightness of the force which sustains, moves and directs this most subtle element.

"I gazed in glad wonder, for I had often endeavored to penetrate the secret, in my researches and investigations. Now was I brought face to face with the Master of the Winds, which give impetus and force to all life upon this planet, whether it be a mineral, plant or animal. Everything which hath increase or decrease upon the earth is under the control of the Master of the Winds. He knows how the Universe was builded.

They who seek knowledge and potency, must yield allegiance, devoid of fear, to this ruler. By so doing they can receive power to control the visible, and to be served by those who constitute the armies of this mighty realm.

"The Ancient One smiled benignantly upon me, saying: 'I perceive thou knowest from thine own understanding, the thing I would say to thee. Art thou willing to be tried? Weigh well thine answer, for thy spirit must not quail, nor thy courage fail thee in the supreme moment of trial, lest thy physical be unable to bear up under the weight infringing upon it, and thou wilt be overcome by the immensity of thine own inviting.'

"I felt no drawing back, nor shrinking. My reply to the questioning was :

"'I am ready to be tried, whenever it shall please those who have the matter in charge. For this purpose am I here."

"'It is well,' was the reply. 'To-morrow thou wilt commence thy preparation.' And then the moonbeams enveiled him in their brightness, until he could no longer be perceived.

"So on the morrow, obedient to the voice and instruction of my Guru, I commenced a system of practicing in breathing, which includes inspiration, expiration and explosion; this latter modified is audible speech. Explanation was also made to me, how voice and speech were vibration manifested. All sound was vibration, either primary or secondary. The condition of the Universe at any given point depended upon vibration. Little by little, I came to the full knowledge and understanding of the manifestation of the Spirit of the Air. Still more, I perceived the powers and potencies belonging to him as one of the Seven Great Rulers, who carry out the creative thought of the Causeless Cause.

"At the end of my time of preparation, I had control of my breath, either to increase or withhold, thereby making myself master of my physical manifested life. The last three days were spent in repose, not fasting, but in full flow of normal life, that there should be no diminution of the reserved bodily strength needed to endure the trial that must precede the ceremony of initiation.

"A little before midnight, I was aroused from sleep by my Guru, and two attendants. They handed me a garment, brilliantly white from self-effulgent light. This fitted my whole form exactly and seemed to add to its strength and suppleness. A pair of sandals, fitting so closely to the feet as to be removed only by the exertion of much force, were next put on. Although my whole dress fitted me thus perfectly, it did not in any way impede the circulation or confine the muscles. Over all was thrown an Egyptian peplos or outer garment, of pure white linen.

"Thus arrayed, I walked forth with my

companions, from my chamber. As, through numberless narrow and winding passages, we went down deeper and deeper into the bowels of the earth, my Guru said:

"'My brother, for the first time thou dost essay thine unaided strength in conflict. Thou hast matured and ripened. Further advance can come only through thyself. Hitherto, we have been able to inspire and protect thee in the Supreme moment, if thou shouldest have needed it. But as thou didst not, we have allowed thee to move forward, until thou art now about to prove, alone and unaided, thine own power. If thou dost prevail, we can still help thee. If thou dost fail, we shall be powerless to assist, until the demands of him, whose territory thou dost invade are satisfied. Be brave. Be vigilant. If fear overtakes thee, thou art lost. If thou art in a strait, look up to thy Higher Self, and gather there from the inexhaustible supplies whatever thou shalt have need of.'

"Here he paused, embraced me, and turning back, left me in charge of the attendants. We, going forward, penetrated yet deeper into the earth.

"At last, the narrow passage broadened into a cave, high-arched, the floor being rock, smooth and firm. Opposite the entrance, at the farther end of the cave, by some convulsion of nature, a clean split from top to bottom had been made, leaving an immense chasm, whose height and depth, length and breadth, were hidden in impenetrable darkness.

"Midway between the entrance and the great cleft, my attendants stopped.

"'Lay aside thy cloak,' said one.

"I, accordingly, took off my outer wrapping, and immediately the light from the under garment I wore flamed out, actually pushing back the darkness, and making all things visible.

"'Now,' said the other attendant, ' approach the Cave of the Winds. If thou dost hear plainly the voice of thy Guru, hesitate not, but obey. Let thy knowledge and thy courage direct thee. When thou dost return, we shall be here to re-conduct thee to those thou lovest.'

"Ever since we had come within hearing distance, moans and groans, and blood-curdling screams, and inarticulate, gibbering sounds, like the laughter of idiots and madmen, had, without ceasing, welled up out of the blackness. Now, as I approached the chasm, they increased, as if all the horrible sounds ever made upon the earth were here collected. Their concentration was appalling in its awful intensity of terror, even to the stoutest heart. While my physical shrank, there was not the slightest shade of fear resting on my Spirit, my real self. But high borne and dominant, I stood at last upon the terrific brink, amidst the dreadful clamor. I could now perceive an immense tidal rush of enormous volume, underlying or emitting the sounds so overwhelming, so confusing. But passing beyond physical sense, my spirit reached the smooth flow of the astral currents. To the inner sense came the voice of my Guru, clearly, and in even tones, a voice I could never mistake:

"'With all thy strength leap forward.'

"I waited not. Gathering all my force, I sprang out into the darkness.

"To say that I expected anything one way or another would not be true. I was content to obey, without theorizing or questioning. As I leaped out, I sank rapidly into the abyss as if falling, but was soon aware of being upborne by mighty hands, while constantly and rapidly descending. It seemed ages that I was descending, the din about me still continuing in all its appalling awfulness.

"I noticed, also, that my descent was on the line of the circumference of a circle. How long I descended I know not. I felt perfectly at ease, and saw simply the periphery of my own body, by its self-diffused light. The descent ended, then followed a short lull, as if in almost lateral motion I was passing the lower dead point of force. This was followed by the upward sweep of the ascending arc, but all noise had ceased. Instead, there was a silence as fearful to bear as the clamor had been; and the feeling of solitude and utter loneliness such as one experiences in a desert, when widely separated from human companionship.

"It was curious that neither here nor elsewhere

during the revolutions was I at all concerned about my condition or position. I simply noted events as so much matter for increased knowledge in the future. Still I moved up, up, until light broke through the darkness; not full light but like a great spear piercing the gloom, which stubbornly held its ground as its against opponent.

"Again I descended, but was now aware of moving in a circle of shortened diameter, and when motion ceased, I found myself standing erect on a small space of blackness, so intense, so dark, as to afford firm footing. I felt fresh, vigorous and undismayed as I waited patiently for further unrolling. Nor waited I long.

"Again came the voice of my Guru: ' Thou hast done well. The Spirit of the Air is upon thee. Thou canst conquer, not by physical strength but by the persistent dominance of thy will.'

"Hardly had his words ceased, when there stood before me an athlete, resembling myself in every particular, as if he were my reflection in a mirror. He approached me and in musical accents, said:

"'Mortal, thou hast penetrated into my audience chamber. What dost thou seek?'

"A voice like my own, but not my own, speaking the thought which might have been a dream, so far off did it seem, replied:

"'Spirit of the Air, I seek from thee the password to the inner Chamber of the Neophytes.'

"'But I have sworn by myself, as a Builder of the Universe, never to impart the secret to an inferior. Wilt thou try thy strength with me?'

"Again, my Higher Self answering for me, said:

"'Oh, Spirit of the Air, thou wast ever capricious and subtle, but in fairness and truth, as thou hast made it, so do I accept thy offer. If thou dost not overcome me, thou wilt grant my boon? Swear it by thyself.'

"And the Spirit of the Air replied:

"'I swear it by myself as one of the Seven Builders. Witness ye, all my hosts.'

"A murmur out of the darkness, like the voice of ten thousand times ten thousand, and thousands upon thousands, gave answer:

"'We witness thy oath.'

"We locked arms, and as we wrestled, I could feel at one moment the icy breath of the frozen poles. Then would sweep down upon me the scorching, debilitating blasts of the desert sirocco. I realized the foresight of those who had given me the apparel of protection. * Up and down, sidewise, and in constant contortion, more or less violent, we exerted our utmost strength, but he prevailed not, for I felt constantly, unremittingly, the impulse, ' I will not be overcome.'

"Thus went on the trial, until a silvery voice that pervaded space, instead of coming from a single point, said:

"'Cease, Spirit of the Air. Thou hast not conquered. Give to the seeker, the thing he seeks.'

"And the Spirit of the Air, smiling upon me, in gentle tones promised thus:

"Mortal, thou hast been a worthy antagonist, and I congratulate thee for thy courage and endurance, and also the Brotherhood who have thee in training. When thou shalt have need thereof, the password will be in thy possession.' Saying this, he laid his left hand just under the base of my brain. Darkness closed in upon me. For a single fraction of a second it seemed as if it would suffocate me. Then a wavering, a relaxing, and a lifting of the shadows, and I find myself standing erect with my two attendants.

"'Welcome, thou who hast been tried and found worthy. Receive refreshment for thy physical.' Saying this, one of my companions took from his girdle a small, curiously wrought flask, filled with a colorless liquid, and gave it to me.

"'Drink,' he said. I drank, and in an instant felt relieved of all the fatigue of the long struggle.

"'How long have I been gone?' I questioned.

"'It is almost low twelve of the second day,' was the reply. ' But we must hasten hence, to the Chamber of the Neophytes.'

"Clothed again in my outer garment, and accompanied by my attendants, who, members of the Brotherhood, deemed it an honor to assist him who was weaker than themselves, I followed the winding passages to the never-to-be forgotten Hall of Obligation, whose doors opened noiselessly, as we ascended the seven steps leading up to its ample portals.

"Only a faint light now illumined it. Although apparently unoccupied, the feeling of overmastering presence continually dwelling there, could not be evaded or put aside. I noticed at the further end of the hall, now appeared a flight of five steps, leading to the door of the Chamber, before which a sentinel holding a gleaming sword kept guard and watch.

"Again throwing aside my outer garment, and clad as in the trial, I approached the Sentinel.

"'Stand, bold intruder,' challenged the Sentinel. ' This is the Chamber of the Neophyte. No one can enter without the Pass of the Builders, which worth alone can obtain. Hast thou the Pass? '

"On my replying in the affirmative, he said: ' Advance and give it to me.' I stepped closer, and in low breath gave the syllables that came voluntarily to my lips. Syllables I can never forget.

"'The pass is correct. Enter and partake of that which belongs to thee.'

"The door slid to one side, soundlessly. Within I see a Hall, in its general outline resembling the Hall of Obligation, but smaller. About one-third of the distance across, from where I stand, is a throne. Before this throne is an altar. Over the center of the altar is suspended, without any visible support, a circle of brilliant, white light, enclosing a six-pointed star, also intense in its brightness. The circle revolving on its diameter, now slow, now fast, gave the appearance of a globe of fire. The more slowly it moved, the more brilliant and steady was its light. When the motion increased, the light became wavering and coruscating in all its prismatic hues, gradually withdrawing into itself as the speed increased, until a central orb of splendor alone remained. Then as the motion fell off, it would again flash out brilliant alike in all its parts, like the rapidly unfolding bloom of some tropical flower.

"Behind the altar, upon the throne, sat the awful presence, its outline clearly defined, impalpable and veiled above the shoulders with a still more visible mistiness. From the place where the eyes would be, came a scintillating, piercing gleam, not perceptible by personal sense, but manifest to the soul sense, and conveying all the sensations as if on the physical plane, only a thousand-fold more intense, even as the invisible rays of heat are more powerful than the visible rays of light. I did not fear. I felt overshadowed by the superior, who brooked no equal. My spirit offered rightful homage to whom homage belonged. It was not the homage of blind obedience, but the sincere regard of a loving heart for one who had attained.

"Beyond the throne, in semi-circle, sat the

Brotherhood of the temple, veiled, and clad in pure white robes. Beyond them, was an arched doorway, overhung by a curtain of the richest, heaviest fabric wrought in gold, and sparkling with the most precious stones, whose surfaces reflected in a constant kaleidoscopic succession, the ever moving light on the altar.

"The walls were ceiled with a fragrant wood, dark and highly polished. On these, as on a mirror, were reflected curious images, which came as the pictures come out of the frost upon the glass, and disappeared, only to be followed by others at intervals. These were reflections from the astral light.

"All these things I saw as I advanced to the altar, where I knelt for further instruction. In the space above pealed out sonorously in clear, silvery tones, the strokes of a bell, but no bell was visible there. I counted the strokes. It noted the hour of low twelve. As the last stroke pealed out upon the air, the garnet, which hung upon my neck in full sight, seemed to Haze out with a new lustre, enveloping me in an aura, emanating from myself. An indescribable fragrance, appealing at once to the smell and taste, diffused itself through the Chamber. The Brotherhood as one rose to their feet. The voice of the Unseen Presence, in its soul-penetrating sweetness, came to my inner sense:

"' My brother, for a second time hast thou, by the Right Way, sought the altar of obligation. Thy devotion and sacrifice are accepted. We gladly offer the, two-fold bond, which, while it makes you more closely one of ourselves, obligates us more firmly to befriend and watch over you. Stand erect, and repeat the obligation of the Neophyte, that binds thee to a closer union, at once with thy Higher Self, and with all the Brotherhood.'

"Standing erect, as a perfect man, I slowly and distinctly repeated the vow of the Neophyte, that through all the aeons to come, is at once his pledge of fealty and his assurance of assistance from the Brotherhood, anywhere, at any time. As the last words of adjuration fell from my lips, the far-off voice of a multitude whom no man could number, uttered these words:

"'As thou art bound to us, so are we, the Brotherhood,, of all the ages, bound to thee. As thou dost remember thy pledge, so will we remember ours.'

"The manifestation of presence lessened. The brothers came up and greeted me, and my Guru said: ' Retire now to thy chamber, for the day already brightens the East. Three days hence, I will come to thee.'

"On reaching my chamber, I flung myself upon my couch, and passed out into sleep, which for two days and nights held me. On the morning of the third day, as the rising sun burnished the walls of my chamber, I awoke. My usual attendants were in waiting. In going into my bath, it was on my mind to divest myself of my luminous garment and sandals. To my astonishment, nothing of the kind was visible upon my person. No trace of any foreign substance remained upon the skin, but that itself was changed. It glowed, in its perfection and suppleness, like that of a trained gladiator. My whole physical was inspired with a new vigor, and my soul wrought up to accomplish the highest aims. These garments could not have been taken from me without my knowledge. I have no explanation to offer.

"As the day waned, my Guru came and we talked of the things I could understand. As when one, going up a mountain, sees a broader horizon, new perceptions of things I supposed I had understood, dawned upon me, and things I had not dreamed of became perceptible.

"As we chatted, a third person, without announcement, sat with us. My Guru smiled, while I, looking intently, recognized the astral form of my wife.

"Turning to me, she said: 'My lord, I congratulate thee, in that thou hast been proved worthy. As the Senor, your Guru, will tell thee, I have also reached the degree of the Neophyte in the Orient. I am really and truly thy brother. We are two points in the line of common union of all who love the truth. Now, more and more closely united shall we become in our search for the " Pearl of great price." Disturb not thyself, for I am under the care of our brothers, and shall again meet thee, when being duly rested and refreshed, thou wilt return to sunny Spain. Remember, my lord, we are ONE, from ages past, and can never more be separated.'

"I glanced at my Guru a single instant, as if he had addressed me, and looking back where my wife had sat, we were alone. My feeling of appreciation for her whom I loved so truly in the highest, best sense of that word, could not find expression in words. It was so like her kind thoughtfulness, to inform me by word of mouth of that which it was so pleasant for me to hear.

"It is wonderful how much of man's narrowness and selfishness falls away, as soon as the element of time is eliminated from his calculations of existence. If accomplishment is only sure sometime, there is no need of the whirl and excitement of impatient worry and uneasy fretfulness. He cannot wait for the ripening of the times and seasons. As my Guru said:

"'The lesson to learn, is the well-doing of the present duty. This involves the perfection of the duty that shall follow. A good foundation makes solid the whole superstructure of the edifice.'

"Day after day, in the temple and in the gardens, for I, having no desire for droneship, insisted that tasks should be assigned me there, such as were assumed by others, I grew harmonious with the great thought currents of the Universe. In the twilight hours, the ever quiet tones of my Guru stimulated my thought, broadened my vision, and lighted up all the unrolling panorama of life, with a more lasting radiance. Sometimes, under the touch of his understanding, the heavens opened, and the glimpses of their wonders and glories left me eagerly desirous for more.

"Thus passed the months, until the day for my departure had come. All things being in readiness, and sure of my return, I was not dismayed at the prospect before me. My Guru, coming to me as the day fell away, said:

"'My brother, you go hence for another seven years' experience with the world. You will do all the good you can, where it is the most needed, because you love to do it. I see for you persecution and unjust punishment. Take this, for a talisman, from me, should you need sadden help.' Saying this, he handed me a beautiful sapphire ring, in which the stone was held in the jaws of a small dragon, whose body and tail completed the circlet.

"'Whenever in your need you shall look upon this, and pronounce the pass of the Neophyte, you will at once receive help equal to your necessity, from the Brotherhood, visible and invisible. Your work you know. Outside the gate you will find your horse. Mount and ride. When you have reached a point within fifty miles of the port whither thou goest, there will come to thee from the Southwest, a messenger bearing dispatches. Whatsoever he knows thou also shalt know of the king's business, which has been ably transacted. Now, farewell!'

"Thus affectionately we parted, as he handed me through the wicket. I stepped to the side of the horse, now becoming quite an old friend, mounted, the gate closed, and for a second time. my face was set toward the world, for which I had so little desire.

"I settled back in my saddle. The feeling of sustaining, of upbearing, had fully possessed me. Ever more should I rely implicitly upon those whose power, reaching everywhere, upon the earth and in the heavens, had sworn to be my shield and guide in all my acts intended for the good of all, regardless of self. Neither time nor space would any longer be units of measurement for me, but that which I had to do for the good would be compared with what I did, for it must all be done.

"With a feeling of rest, therefore, I settled back in the saddle.

"The movements of my horse were like the pulsations of a heart-beat. The rush of the air past me was like the flowing of a torrent. At the appointed place, I found a horse and rider, the very counterpart of myself, awaiting me. A packet of papers was handed me. I busied myself for a moment arranging them upon my person. When I raised my eyes to accost the courier, there was neither horse nor rider. Nor had the speed of my own steed slackened by so much as a single hoof-beat.

"A curious sense of double consciousness possessed me for a few moments. This merged into a feeling of oneness again. Then a vision or dream of certain things having transpired during the past year, which became certain knowledge when the perusal of the papers on shipboard confirmed all that I had mentally received. This, the final unfoldment fully corroborated. It was the king's business, which had been most skillfully and successfully transacted, and I was to be allowed to make a favorable report.

"As the day dawned, my horse stopped, and left me in the same place, where, seven years before, he had vanished from my sight. I sought the sentry, and had now no difficulty, as a courier of the king, in reaching the commandant. His slight curiosity was allayed by the explanation, confirmed by my packet of papers, that I had been sent on a secret mission. In those days Spanish officers asked few questions, and obeyed orders implicitly.

"It was but a short time, when one of the treasure ships homeward bound, dropped anchor in the bay, seeking supplies. It was an easy task to secure passage. The captain said he had heard of my exploits and daring deeds and that I was reputed to bear a charmed life in the country to which I had been sent, and that my success as a diplomat was also famous. I did not tell him what news this was to me, but simply disclaimed the whole, only to be considered modest in the matter. But I knew that an agent of the Brotherhood had been acting for me in the king's business, under orders. He had succeeded far better than I could have even hoped to do. It was not necessary that I should offer explanations to those who could not understand.

"The homeward voyage was swift and prosperous. On my arrival I sought immediate audience with the king, who, although pleased with the outcome of the public business, was evidently both surprised and puzzled that I should have been successful; and by no means pleased to see me returned to disquiet him by my presence.

"After the details of the business had been duly explained, I begged the boon of retirement to my estate. With ill-concealed satisfaction the favor was granted. I left the royal presence once more, glad that I was protected against malice and hypocrisy.

"On reaching my chateau, I found my wife eagerly anxious for my arrival, her face bright with gladness at my safe return. After a few days of restful quiet, we compared notes, as to the initiations we had passed through. All was similar, save in her case the trial was one of fortitude of soul, without the call for physical strength. In this she had overcome, and won that which she had sought. Our mutual comparison of experience was both instructive and gratifying.

"I need not enter into details of the events of the swift passing years. Sufficient to say that our studies and the care of the estate filled full all my time, and having risen above the plane of anxiety, life was very pleasant.

CHAPTER VII.

SIX YEARS HAD PASSED. I had attained quite a reputation for my skill in healing disease, which had latterly come to me as a gift, one of the results of persistent advance in the line of occult knowledge. Many of the cures were so remarkable that I was looked upon by the ignorant with awe and some little distrust, lest my power should be outside the lines of the Catholic Church. My reputation as a leech had extended even to the Capital. I knew it had spread through spies, by whom the king had kept himself informed of all the outside world knew of my daily acts and pursuits. So long as they had no political significance he had not cared to molest me.

"But on the day of which I now speak, a courier from the Capital announced that the plague had broken out at Madrid, and the king summoned me to try my skill in controlling it.

"Knowing that out of this small beginning a long train of consequences would evolve, I retired to my laboratory and sought advice from my Guru. Fixing my thought on the far-off, the astral presence soon responded, and his low, strength-inspiring tones said:

"'My brother, I see thou dost not question as to the opportunity to help thy fellows, but simply desirest instruction as to how it can best be accomplished. Further, thou seekest to know the best manner in which it may be expedient for thee to move in the matter. It is well. Hesitate not to obey the king's behest, but when in the days to come he shall seek thy life, the Brotherhood will protect thee. It is all so written in thy line of life. Thy strength shall be according to thy burdens. Bid thy wife farewell for an indefinite period, for like the revolving circles, your lives cease to run parallel until such time as the tasks before each shall be completed.'

"Preparations were made. With a long embrace and caress my wife and myself parted, not inconsolable, but relying on the promises of those who had never thus far failed us, that we should again be united, when that which was set for us to do should be accomplished.

"Arriving at the Capital, I reported at the palace, where I found confusion and dismay on every hand. All audience was denied. Finding there was no head to affairs but fear, I went forth to the most loathsome part of the city and commenced my career. My success was wonderful. It seemed as if the sick in the lazar- houses had but to hear my words, to look upon my presence, in order to bring healing to themselves, so mighty was the manifestation of the power of the Brotherhood through me. Nor did my powers decrease as the days went by. Through me the Brotherhood interposing a barrier stayed the plague.

"I was hailed as a deliverer, a friend of all. My reputation brought me a large practice, from which I could not escape, even if I desired selfishly to lay down the burden. Really, not for myself, but for the sake of those in need and distress, I worked on.

"My growing popularity alarmed the king, and disturbed the physicians, who declared I had no right to practice medicine, because I had never studied at the schools. The king sought means to stop the outward expression. They were not far off.

"One night, three black-robed figures, in the usual manner, arrested me at my lodgings. Within an hour I was occupying a cell of the Spanish Inquisition, that realized hell of man's imagination. When brought before the infernal tribunal I was accused of practicing the Black Art. My success in alleviating the miseries of mankind, was declared to be the work of the devil, with whom I most be in league.

"I confessed that I was not an educated physician, and that my success in healing was due to a superior power, but naught else could they extort from me. Because I would not say that good was evil, and declare myself worthy of death, I was sentenced to torture.

"On the morrow my sentence was to be carried out. Lying upon the rude pallet in my cell, meditating upon the injustice of man to his fellow, it occurred to me that he had no right to injure nor maim another, under any pretext whatsoever, and that I was not called upon to endure torture of any kind, least of all, from those who used religious pretense to cloak selfish purposes. My eyes fell upon the sapphire ring upon my finger. Its pale, blue light kindled under my gaze and streamed out in penetrating potency. The parting instructions of my Guru recurred to my mind, with startling distinctness. Those wonderful words, the pass of the Neophyte, offered themselves plainly, and were gravely, reverently spoken, out into the silence, for the first time audibly in almost seven years, since before the door of the Temple Chamber I had received them. Almost seven years. Days and nights had been so crowded with events, since I came to the Capital that the nearness of the end of my probation had passed from my memory.

"No sooner had the first sound vibrated upon the air, than a presence formulated itself before me, and as I finished, one of the brothers, whom I knew well, stood in my cell.

"'Thy Guru hath requested me to come for thee. It is time thou didst turn thy face towards those who lovingly wait for thee, and truly desire thy welfare.

"'Robe thyself for the outside world, take this staff, and let us go hence.' I at once put on my garments, and taking the staff he offered me, was ready to accompany him. The immense triple-locked doors of the great prison of the Inquisition opened for us. Neither keeper nor sentinel offered obstruction to our progress. The darkness veiled us. At the outskirts of the city, we found horses waiting us. Mounting, we rode rapidly Westward. On a spur of the Sierra de Gata we halted a few moments, not because of the need of our animals, for they were as fresh as when we started, but because I desired to look over the broad country that had brought so much of sorrow, and so little of joy to me.

"'My brother,' said my companion, look thy last upon ingrate Spain, whose dust thou now shakest from thy feet forever. A hard and bitter mother has she been to thee. But that which she had to do for thee and that which thou hadst to do for her is this day finished.'

"Although I felt it to be true that Spain had been only a fierce, exacting protector, yet the force of the love I had cherished for her, gave a shade of regret to this, the final parting. I have since been in all the countries of the earth, and in the Spanish colonial possessions, bat I have never, since that time, entered the boundaries of the mother country. We crossed Portugal swiftly without hindrance or delay, from any source whatever.

"Arrived at the seaboard on the summit of one of the mountains of the coast range, at my companion's suggestion we dismounted. As we stepped away to refresh our cramped limbs after our long ride, our horses vanished into thin air. I looked at my companion. He was standing erect with his face toward the West. A peculiar look of concentrated potency overspread his features. As I watched him and noticed the hardening of all the lines of his face, my eye involuntarily followed his line of projection into the Western horizon. In the far-off sky I noticed first, a tiny speck which gradually enlarged until there rested upon the slope at our feet, an air yacht, complete in all its appointments.

"My companion motioned me to step on board, and he followed, taking the helm himself. Obeying the impulse of his intelligence, the yacht swung around, her immense sail filled before a strong breeze from the East. Without the friction of resisting matter, moving at the same speed as the wind, we were on our journey, like an arrow from the bow. Far beneath us lay the ocean and the clouds.

"'My brother,' I questioned, 'whence comes this vessel?'

"'Oh!' he replied, ' it is one of the models laid up in the astral light, from the thought of the Old Atlantians. Some day, some of the clear-sighted earth-born will see it, and have knowledge and power enough to manifest it for themselves. Meanwhile it will continue in its store-house, except when it may be used as we are now using it. All the inventions of the earth-born are made in this way. They are discovered in the sense that one discovers a sail on the ocean. But in the sense of creation from nothing, never.'

"'Why could I not have come to you in this way, on my previous trips?' I asked.

"'Because you had not sufficient soul-unfoldment,' was the reply. 'Now, you do not depend upon other force than your own potency. Of this you are fully self-conscious. This makes you calm, and evenly poised. Seven years ago this was not so. It employs the utmost measure of my own will power, to hold our vessel in manifestation. If I were required to hold you up also, with an uncertain and varying amount of sustaining, we might suddenly find ourselves wrecked.'

"Thus whiling away the time in conversation, we swept on and on, until at length far beneath us, could be seen the outlines of the old fort. We lingered not here, but with unslackened velocity sped forward, to find ourselves, at last, at the crest of the mountains towering over the Temple. Here our craft beached, and swung broadside to, for us to disembark.

"My companion said: ' You know the way down

into the gardens, where I will join you as soon as I have re-assumed my outer garment of flesh.'

"Following his direction, I soon found myself in company with my brothers, whose quaint, kind words of joy, had more gladness for me than any other human thing. We were soon joined by the brother, under whose guidance I had made my recent journey. He did not seem in any wise discomfitted by his late absence from his body.

"Best and refreshment were my most urgent needs. The next day my Guru said: 'My brother, seven months of preparation lie before thee, and then comes your final trial. If successful, more worlds than this lie at your feet. But remember that even great ones fall back from the threshold. Beware of feeling unduly uplifted by self-consciousness, at the present position.'

"I had not dreamed this to be possible. I had never, from the first hour of my entrance into the Temple, indulged in any hopes for the future yet to come, after reaching this or that point. My only formulated hope was, that some day it might be my lot to share the life of the Brothers in the Temple. I only thought of this, as it might be worthily won by me as a right, and not in any sense as an usurpation of another's rights or place. But I was glad of my Guru's suggestion, for it set me to examining myself in the secret thought, and to the striving for the obliteration of any and all taint of selfishness.

"A large part of the days of preparation were spent in the practice of controlling the action of nature in the formation and shaping of the inanimate, inorganic combinations of the element called matter. This will always respond to the vibrations of thought, if we know how to project our potency of Will. All things are One, from one source. The hints of the ability to transmute one metal into another, are not idle suggestions. That which has been once created by the Infinite Thought of the Universe, can also be changed and transformed, under the same law, by the finite thought.

"I was more fully taught, that as I was one with the whole Universe, I could neither disturb nor injure another without affecting myself. He who suffers most from selfishness, is the one who is selfish, seeking only his own ends regardless of the desires or good of others. It was also deeply impressed upon my mind that, having eliminated the selfishness that springs from, and is coordinate with, manifestation on the physical plane, one could only hope to reach full attainment by striving to comprehend, in all its fullness, the fact that the Higher Self is not now, nor can be separate from the One Absolute Self. Whenever this is wholly comprehended, then man, even on the physical plane, can become 'one of us,' the Adonai, Elohim or Devas. Once having won his way into the ranks of the Brotherhood in its highest degree, he is entitled to the harmony of the whole, and the protection and assistance of every member. Again and again during the months of preparation, were these truths brought clearly and forcibly to my mind, until they became certain convictions.

"In my hours of meditation, I was bidden to reflect on the One, the Causeless Cause ; and to let the thought of its immensity overshadow me, but in no way to imagine either possibility or power of equality. But by dwelling upon It, in its unknowability, my own spirit should be strengthened, and my soul force be quickened and stirred to its utmost power, and thus hold in leash the physical, to respond promptly when the hour of trial should strike.

"Thus, through the short seven months, my training went forward, I knew I was growing stronger, and also that my self-abnegation, my desire to benefit all the world, entirely regardless of any consequences, or reflex action on myself, was becoming an impelling motive of my every action. All the petty distinction of friend or foe, or of family ties, ceased to exercise any binding force. In all the Universe, there could be to me only those who had attained to the Brotherhood, and those who had not, but might if they would. To these last the hand of help was always to be extended, in all tenderness and love.

"One should first seek to inspire them with a desire to advance out of the darkness of ignorance, because without this no gain can be permanent.

"The last month of preparation was devoted to physical training. My Guru said:

"'The perfect man must be perfect, both physically and spiritually. That is, the body must, if the training were correct, be the manifestation of the correct currents flowing from within, and be a reflection of the right thought. As you have reached the point where the body is to receive its last trial, it must be possessed of its utmost vigor.'

"At last, dawned the day of days. As the first glimmer of light brightened the Eastern sky, my Guru came to me, bade me rise and accompany him. Having dressed myself, myself, we went forth from my chamber together. Instead of descending, we went out upon a level through a passage that led us to an immense plateau. As we went on my Guru said:

"'Your trial is now two-fold. It will require all your strength of body and soul. The first half must take place beyond our boundary. Neither I, nor any of the Brotherhood, will in physical form attend you. But you know our powers are not limited to these bounds. Those who serve us are also beyond, as well as with us. Into trusty hands we shall commit you, and our undivided attention will be given you, during your trial. If thou hast need use this call.' Here he whispered a word of potency in my ear. ' It will give to thee immediate and supporting strength.' As he spoke, the passage through which we were moving opened, by a sudden turn into the sunlight.

"Here we paused. I saw my Guru's lips move. Then two men, huge of stature and massive in muscle, came into the passage. They respectfully saluted my Guru and awaited orders.

"'Into thy hands, oh, faithful and tried,' said he,' I commit our brother, who by obedience to the law, seeks to reach that which the law holds for him, in common with all disciples.' The strangers bowed, and my Guru, with a grave smile, turned back whence he came, while I went forward into the light of the new day, with my two friends.

"When we had reached the outer air we stood on a beach of sand, within an old volcanic crater of immense size. It was almost a perfect circle in form, with a bench of sandy beach running two-thirds of the way about it, and beyond that the lake placid and unruffled. On its surface was no ripple. No sound, nor motion, came from its unknown depths. Standing upon its brink, with my attendants, they said :

"'At the bottom of this pool lies thy way. Stand still, and listen for the voice of the Unseen.'

"Obeying my instructors, I stood once more quiet as to my body, and introverted as to my spiritual sense. From out the silence came to my perception the voice of him, I had so often heard, in assurance:

"'Divest thyself of thy apparel, and seek by thy strength, the bottom of the pool. Waste not thy force, but use judiciously, reserving for the final effort.'

"With not a single moment's hesitation, I stripped off my wrappings, and plunged head first into the pool. I was considered an excellent swimmer, and my training of the last few months had made available every fibre of my body. But I could not reach the bottom and soon found myself floating upon the surface again. Once more I essayed to reach the bottom and failed. Still undismayed, for the third time I made the attempt, and now all that constitutes the man, was concentered in the action. Not a single atom of the physical, not a single idea of spirit potency that was not wholly intent on the one purpose. This time, the waters, feeling the full imperiousness of accomplishment, seemed to cleave asunder of their own accord. When I reached the golden sands at the bottom they, too, opened. The direction of my movement was now reversed ; instead of being head down I was coming up, apparently, through the cleft at the bottom into a pellucid pool, in an immense grotto.

"Swimming to the shore, I found it covered with soft moss. Here, exhausted, I stretched myself at full length, for a few moment's rest. Rousing myself from the semi-trance condition in which I was plunged at the Supreme moment

I noted the sensation of quiet and rest and then fell asleep.

"From this condition of lethargy, I was aroused by the sound of musical voices in soft cadence. Rising to a sitting posture, a little group of water nymphs, not far from me, perceived I had wakened, and came towards me. Beautiful in form, and lovely in all that word implies, I could not but admire, as it is a man's privilege to admire, anything and everything upon the earth, without a craving for possession.

"Having approached me, the stateliest one of the group thus accosted me:

"'Oh, mortal-born! what dost thou seek in the realm of the "Spirit of the Water?"'

"A voice, not of myself, but still seeming myself, made answer: 'Fair nymphs, I seek audience with the Spirit of the Water, and I crave from you the boon of speedily furthering my wishes.'

"'But why hasten?' was her reply. 'You may dwell with us. Are we not fair In feature and beautiful in form? Doth not that always suffice the mortal-born?'

"And my Higher Self made answer: 'Thou sayest but too truly, Daughter of the King. These things do satisfy the mortal-born, but when he has been regenerated of the water and the fire, the continual attainment of that which lies beyond is the only source of content.'

"'But the way you seek to travel is beset with

dangers. Strong, bold men have perished there, and we would save thee from their doom.'

"'But what would be the doom of him who proves recreant to his vows?'

"Thou hast thus far accomplished, Oh Mortal! Be satisfied and seek nothing beyond.'

"'I thank you for your interest in me, but do not seek to detain me. Show yourselves the friends you claim to be, by helping me to that which I seek.'

"Tender indeed were the speaker's accents now: ' If thou wilt not be dissuaded from thy danger, then will we help you to the utmost of our power.'

"As she finished speaking, it grew dark. There was a motion as of all my environment at once, just as if one were borne on the midst of a deep sea current. A little while and the motion ceased. The darkness unfolded, and I found myself reclining in a large hall, scooped out of the adamantine rocks, by the moving waters. There were many forms flitting all about me, incessantly coming and going on the business to which they were set. From here, the tides were managed, and the springs of the earth maintained. From here, was regulated the rush of the mountain torrents, and the mighty rivers were guided and renewed in their flow. Here, also, was the manufactory of the dews and rains, and the controlling power by which their supply was equalized throughout the seasons.

"All the attendants, in their pre-occupation ignored my presence. I had only time for a short glance about me. Near where I was reclining, a throne of white marble, fantastically carved, rose from the rock floor to an imposing height, and shone with an inherent light, resembling the phosphorescent glow of the sea, but steadier and brighter in its action. Upon the upper table of the structure, rested a huge shell, whose clear surface of pearl glistened even beneath the fabric of sea silk, upon which sat half-reclining, a dwarf, perfect -in his form and proportions. His long, white beard flowed to his feet, but his dark eyes, though piercing, were kindly.

"As his glance fell upon me, I arose, and kneeling at the foot of the throne, I heard his words:

"'Stranger, of the earth-born, what seekest thou in the palace of the Spirit of the Water? '

"My Higher Self made answer: 'Gracious One, I seek the Hierophant's pass to the Veil of Isis.'

"'Bold mortal! knowest thou not, that I may give thee but two syllables of the pass? The word of words is in the keeping of my brother the Spirit of the Fire, and can only be imparted to him who is found worthy. I am bound by an oath to reveal to him only, who has been fully purified in the physical by water. Many have perished in the trial. The way is long and dangerous. I do not like to see you perish. Stay with us, and do not tempt your fate against what may prove overwhelming odds.'

"'Nay, Oh, Spirit of the Water!' once again answered my Higher Self. 'I thank thee for thy kind words. But thou knowest it would be better to perish striving to attain, than to lie ingloriously, satisfied with partial knowledge. Should I accept your offer, your respect for me' would not be increased.'

"'Thy wisdom doth not fall behind thy attainment. Thou shalt be allowed to have thy wish. Rise and go hence. The nymphs will accompany thee the Hall of Trial. If thy courage fails not, and thou shalt succeed, then that thou dost seek will be in thy possession, and I will be thy servant.'

"He ceased speaking, and the whole Hall filled with a low, sweet melody, like the ripple of laughing waters over a stony bed. Turning to the group of nymphs who stood near. I accompanied them, going by a narrow passage, worn out of the rock, to a large, circular chamber. This room, like all others, here, was the result of the labors of the waters for long, weary years. The sides were of water-worn rocks, dark with age, while underneath, the footsteps fell upon firm, white sand. On the farther side was a large, irregularly shaped opening, in which I could hear the pattering of rain drops on the slightly ascending floor, and beyond that an inexplicable, rushing sound of something heavier and more fear-inspiring.

"Standing before this opening, the elder nymph, who had at the first spoken to me, said, and her tones were sadly tender:

"'Mortal, there lies thy only way to the upper air. Once thou essayest the passage, thou canst never return thither. The great drops thou hearest falling are the salt tears of the world's agony. Once they strike thy body, thou takest upon thyself the burden of the world's sorrow and sin. If thou canst not bear it, then, indeed, thou wilt sink under it, and be crushed by its weight. Or if the pains of passage grow too hard for thee, and mortal pain takes away thy self-possession, thy spirit may need many more bodies to complete its round of perfection. If thou art as strong and fearless as I hope thou art, thou wilt see the sunlight, with the taint of decay and death washed clean from thy physical body, never to return. Be courageous and enduring'—here her eyes grew inexpressibly wistful—' and we may serve thee in all time to come, as the fair delight to honor the brave.'

"I bowed low. 'Fair nymphs, I thank you most sincerely, for your kind interest in my welfare. I pray you, give me in this time of trial your utmost help.'

"Looking upon their faces for the last time, I turned away, and entered the passage. The icy-cold drops, scattered like a spring shower, smote upon my naked body, but with a singular sensation, as if they penetrated beneath the surface of the skin, into the flesh, and with this came a terrible overshadowing and oppression, which no words could describe, for the sorrow and grief therein contained were perfectly inexpressible.

"Still pressing on, my course being slightly upward, the falling water increased in its volume and force of descent, until it seemed to run through my body as if it were a sieve. This downpour became a fierce, rushing torrent, and at the same time I noticed that the temperature was changing from cold to hot. As it grew warmer, there was a sense of compression added to the feeling of the water passing through, instead of over, the surface of my body. Then, lifted off my feet and whirled upward in a vortex, the rapidity of the motion seemed almost to reach the limit of physical endurance. I remembered to keep my arms pressed close to my sides, and my feet together. As thus I shot up, like an arrow from a bow, the heat grew more and more intense. How high the temperature reached, I know not, but I have never experienced anything like it either before or since. When the extreme limit of physical resistance was reached, I was again plunged into a cold stratum. The pain, without my previous training, would have overcome me. I know, also, if fear had added a single feather's weight to the just turning scale of bodily suffering, I should have been lost, crushed by the turbulence of the outer environment.

"With eyes and mouth closed, and breath suspended during the upward rush, I was still in the fullest possession of each and all of the higher principles. I affirmed within myself that which was true, ' I do not fear.' I knew, if I yielded ever so little to physical weakness, I should be overcome. With this thought paramount over all the conditions of sense and mentality, I suddenly found myself hurled into the daylight, in the pool from whence I started, where my guides waited my coming, to congratulate me, or to prepare my body for burial.

"I was myself and yet not myself. By the swell of the water, whose propulsion had shot me forth, I was thrown upon the white sands of the beach, breathless and exhausted. By my astral vision, I perceived the strong, white arms of the water nymph, as she bore me to the care of my friends, her anxiety for me having led her, unseen by my outer self, to accompany my rapid flight to the upper regions.

"My attendants lifted me to my feet, and threw over me a robe of white linen, permeated with a delicate refreshing fragrance. Out of this came new-born strength. I felt wonderfully lightened. The grossness purged away, the body could be stimulated by an aroma, which is the subtile essence of the choicest and best supporters of physical vitality. As a consequence, my mentality worked sharply and clearly.

"On the boundary, I met my Guru and the two Brothers who had previously assisted me. Bidding farewell to those who had served me to the limit of their power in this last struggle, I, again, with my companions, entered the inner chambers of the Temple.

"As we walked slowly along, a sedate joy illumined the face of my Guru, as he said:

"'My brother, it is inexpressible pleasure to behold you thus, with your body in your possession. Yet one more day, and the cleansed and purified physical shall receive a master worthy of itself. Then shall the perfect physical and the perfect spiritual constitute the Perfect man, as was designed by It, whose creative thought was the source of all being.

"'The third day, since you went forth on your mission, has reached high twelve. Retire to thy chamber for refreshment and rest. At low twelve we shall meet again.'

"Obeying his instructions, in my chamber attendants brought me food and drink, such as I had never before seen nor tasted. They were made of the essences, and not the gross elements. So soon as swallowed they were diffused in the new man. A wonderful rehabilitation of power and strength was the immediate result. From that hour, no vileness of either food or drink has passed my lips. My knowledge has enabled me to find suitable substances in the air, in the water, and in the fire. The body is thereby renewed, without wasting a large part of its strength in separating and excreting the waste, which is not, nor never has been, of any use.

"A little before the appointed hour, my Guru came and awakening me from sleep, he said:

"'Thine hour of final attainment is at hand. Rouse thee, and as a man prepare to endure that which seizes hold upon the fountain head of all life and energy.'

"I arose at once, and was soon in readiness to accompany him. Moving along a line of corridors towards the West, we reached at last a circular stairway, cut out of the solid rock, with an opening or well in the center. It was a long distance down. Although neither my Guru nor myself had any of the usual physical means of lighting our way, still all about us there was sufficient light to disclose clearly our immediate neighborhood. I noticed that the walls of solid rock contained great veins of gold. The revenues of an empire were almost constantly in sight, as we descended step by step. These deposits of wealth had been cut through and laid bare, in the process of opening communication with that which we now sought. But all these massed riches ceased to have value, beyond their use, in the eyes of those to whose knowledge it had come. Power to possess had destroyed its precious quality, as it does in all human conditions.

"As I have said, it was a long distance down. I walked on the inner side, next the wall. My Guru took the outer and unprotected side. Below us was darkness. Above us no light could penetrate. The end of the staircase was reached at last. We stopped in a small chamber, which opened into a larger one, and this into a still larger hall, all hewn out of the solid rock.

"As we commenced advancing on a level, I noticed a brightness like the growing dawn of day. This grew brighter and clearer, until, passing into the last hall, I beheld at the farther end, a river and cascade of fire. The light was dazzlingly white, and pained the eyes. There was, however, no heat from it manifest on the outside. While the appearance was that of a river of fire, falling over in a cascade, there was no progressive motion. A difference could be perceived in the continuity of the light, as now it faded, and then grew brilliant again. This was more of a coruscation, than a wavering of strength or intensity.

"Near the entrance, and farthest from the fire, was a couch of stone, slightly inclining from head to feet, and covered with a rug of soft texture. As we entered the hall, six of the Brothers were standing about the couch, conversing in low tones. Arranged in a half oval, facing the fire, the couch occupying one of the *foci,* were seven seats. After greeting the Brothers, all of whom I knew, my Guru bade me recline upon the couch. The brothers took their places upon the stone seats. A moment of silence, and then the voice of my Guru:

"'Lie at ease upon thy back. Introvert thy consciousness, and let go of thy body.'

"Obeying his instructions, I turned upon my back, allowed the muscles to adapt themselves to the surface of the couch, and became passive. Hardly had I done this, before there stole over me a sense of quietness and rest, deepening into unconsciousness. My next sensation was a sound of far-off music, harmonious and intense in its effect, a call to the soul which would take no denial. Then came a sense of full freedom from the circle of necessity. Apparently opening my eyes, I was standing by the couch facing my Guru. In a single glance, I noted my body at rest, in deep sleep upon the couch. I noted also the currents of thought moving in alignment from all the Brothers, and centering where I stood.

"'Thou knowest,' began my Guru, 'thy present condition, for thou hast met thy astral body before. Approach the cascade of fire, and enter boldly therein. Whatever is gross and unassimilable will be consumed, and only thy highest and best will resist the fire, even as fine gold grows brighter, under the fierceness of the flame.'

"I turned toward the cascade leaping and plunging down its rocky bed. As I approached it, moving in all respects as if I were inside, instead of outside, of my physical garment, I noticed that its glow had deepened in its white energy. As I stood at the outer verge, I felt no heat, only a curious sense of constriction, as if one were enclosed in the arms of a mighty wind. The body of the fire hollowed itself out as I came nearer. When I had entered within its bounds, its dimensions grew ample in their enlargement. Seated upon a throne, was a regal figure, of brightness unapproachable, but stern in feature. His questioning glance rested fairly upon me as I drew near.

"'Possessor of a mortal body, what seekest thou in the audience chamber of the Spirit of the Fire?'

"'I seek the word that shall place the Neophyte with power, before the Veil of Isis.'

"'Has thy physical body been purified by the Spirit of the Water, and did it remain in thy possession?'

"'It did, Oh, Spirit of the Fire! But not to me alone, nor to my unaided strength, is the attainment due, but to the help and loving care of the Brotherhood, under whose guidance I have now sought audience with thee, Oh, Implacable!'

"'It is well. If thou hast strength to endure the trial, thy request shall be granted.'

"At this instant, above all, and through all, came the voice of my Guru, more intense in its concentration and soul-inspiring in its modulation, than I had ever deemed possible:

"'Stand erect. Hold with thine utmost will power the thought: "I am, and beside is naught else."'

"I could feel a vivifying influx from the mighty power of the assembled Brothers, and my own will grew invincible, as I affirmed with strongest self-assertion, my consciousness of existence.

"There was no lapse of time in these last three happenings, nor were they in sequence, but came all at once. No sooner had the Spirit of the Fire ceased speaking, than a torrent of flame poured down upon me, in an awfulness which no earthly symbolism nor likeness can in any way portray. As the spirit is the essence of the body, so was this flame the essence of all fire, in its overpowering and almost omnipotent whiteness.

"Even the astral body fused under its fierceness. If at this supreme moment the Spirit should loose its grasp upon the idea of its own entity, and the outline, from any cause, grow dim, then farewell all hope for present attainment—the end comes at once and speedily. I was conscious of the motion, change and rearrangement of soul particles, as the grossness disappeared, and under new polarization the soul itself was born again of the fire, into the purest and the highest possibility.

"During all this focalization of unrestrained force, the astral body did not lose shape, nor become flexed in the slightest degree from its uprightness; for the Will, the Divine Monad, held firmly to the idea of existence. The potency of the affirmation, ' I am,' held even this volatile condition in its place and perfect form, as received in the sequence of Creative Thought.

"There was no feeling of exhaustion, nor diminution, but simply a perception of growing lightness as the dross purged away. There was also a consciousness that whoever ventured here, might without effort on their part disappear entirely.

"But the crisis was passed. The purifying force grew less and less. Once more I stood acquitted, and stronger and purer for the trial. To me, thus the Spirit of the Fire again spoke:

"'It is well, the storm for thee has passed. Return now to thy body, and thy Brothers. When thou dost stand before the Veil of Isis, the pass of the Hierophant, the word that symbolizes the withdrawing and the manifesting, shall be thine. Use it wisely, as thine own spirit shall teach thee, and all will be well. More than mortal! I, too, henceforth and forever serve thee.'

"With swift, gliding motion, hardly conscious how, I stood once more beside my body. Another period of unconsciousness, as lying flat upon the insensible physical, I was absorbed into the outer personality. A shuddering thrill, so forceful as to seem a pain, and I awoke, never more to be the being who had laid down upon the couch; but another, who at all times, and under all circumstances, having put the law of Karma under his feet, could dominate the body.

"As I arose from my resting place, the Brothers also stood up, and coming to me, with quiet gravity, a real gladness in their tones, expressed their delight that I had succeeded.

"'But it was not I, but you, oh, beloved! that made endurance possible. Alone, I never could have held fast to the center of manifested force.'

"'Now,' said my Guru, ' we go once more to the Hall of Obligation. Take due note of all happenings.'

"So we moved on, two by two, out of the light of the Fire, until we had reached the spiral stairway. Here, the Brothers arranged themselves in the order of triumph. First, a single man, then three pairs, of which I was the middle one, nearest the wall, and a single man brought up the rear.

"In all my former exercises and trials, there had been, at the end, the feeling of fasting and exhaustion, but now sustenance and bodily vigor came to me from the air I breathed. I was invigorated by every step I took, by every breath I drew.

"Triumphantly, I stood before the Hall of Obligation. Here my companions left me, my Guru saying:

"'He who lifts the Veil of Isis, must do it alone, by and for himself. Let not thy courage fail thee. Dare to do, to the fullest extent, as thy knowledge shall guide thee.'

*' I ascended the seven steps of the Hall of Obligation, and passed through the wide opening doors. A dim, diffused light permitted me to see my way, as I advanced slowly through the whole length of the Hall. The Presence, as usual, overshadowed me, but now, more than at any previous time, with the intensity of its power.

"Reaching the five steps before the Chamber of the Neophyte, the sentinel held the gates. As the pass of the Neophyte trembled on my lips, the door opened. This Chamber was also vacant, in the visible, but the sense of the overshadowing of the Omnipotent rested upon me. The light was full, so that all objects were clearly discernible.

"About half way across, I was firmly held by invisible forces. Looking upon the polished surface of the room to the right, I noticed the beginning of an unrolling of all the good deeds of all my embodiments from the first incarnation, even to the present hour. On the left, in sequence appeared all the deeds that had brought me discomfort or uneasiness, or pain of mind or body.

"While these manifestations were taking place, each side was reflected in the other, more or less clearly, as either was more or less influential in the on-flowing current of life. A curious intermingling and blending of each into each, was the result. This formed a complete picture of the movement of the lives. Equilibrium was attained by the adjustment of the actions themselves. This is the result of Karmic law. Not all at once, but in the end adjustment was always completed.

"While looking upon this revealing, I had a curious sensation of being part of it, of being at one with it. It was as if the inanimate representation simply reflected the thing I, myself, was; a complex result of actions, and not a unified entity ; the whole overshadowed and held together by an overmastering force of the inner.

Thus was proved to me that the material of the soul, gathered from experiences under the whole heaven and became at one with the Spirit, which is the Word of Power—the Human Will— the Expression of the Divine Energy, constitutes the individual, for the purpose of creating which, 'the Word was made flesh.' As the lesson closed, a voice said to me, plainly:

"'Thy soul is from the Universe; thy Spirit is from the One. As the Universe manifests the One, so thy Soul manifests thy Spirit. Seek and thou shalt find.'

"Released now from the power that had held me for observation, I moved across the Hall and ascending the three steps, stood upon a sort of dais or platform. The heavy veil hung motionless. The light behind it became more and more intense in its brightness, until it seemed to pierce through the meshes of the thickly woven stuff as ordinary sunlight passes through the interstices of thinnest lace.

"As I stepped upon the center of the platform, before the veil, an unseen hand, strong and restraining, was laid upon my shoulder. At the same instant, a tongue of flame, resembling a fiery sword, lay breast high across the outer surface of the curtain.

"'Stand, mortal! who art still under the law,' challenged a voice out of the Unseen, that I recognized as belonging to my Higher Self. ' How hast thou approached the Holy of Holies? Give answer.'

"'By the help of the Brotherhood, and my own obedience,' was my reply.

"'What more dost thou seek?'

"'To lift the Veil of Isis, and thus penetrate all mysteries, both of the Seen and the Unseen ; the animate and the inanimate. To become at one with thee, subtile and untiring questioner. To know what thou knowest, to become as thou art, the unchangeable of the centuries.'

"'Hast thou the pass of the Hierophant?' "'I have.'

"'Then place thyself erect before the Veil of Isis and pronounce it in low breath."

"As I approached closer to the veil, the hand upon my shoulder was lifted, and the flaming barrier dropping its point vanished from sight. For the first time in all the initiations, in my proper self, I, using my own organism, pronounced the sentence that had been so hardly won, syllable by syllable, by me, through endurance and peril.

"Scarcely had my voice in low breath uttered slowly and distinctly the awful words, than intense darkness filled the chamber. The whole mountain quaked. Thunder rolled through the whole Temple. The veil, rent in twain, revealed to my eyes the whiteness of the brightness of the Truth that is Wisdom. Out of the effulgence, came words of exquisite modulation and sweetness. Like the brooding of a dove, they rested on my soul:

"'The peace of the ages abideth with him who has attained. Let thy light shine.'

"Oh! the exaltation and ecstasy of this supreme moment, when the Spirit, perfected by union with the Infinite, and its own Higher Self, claims forever absolute dominion over its perfected body. An enfolding presence wrapped itself about me. The light permeated and became part of myself. Ineffable quiet and rest was the only sensation. To this I yielded fully and entirely.

"It was high twelve of the third day, when I found myself lying upon my couch, in my own chamber.

"In the twilight, my Guru came to me and thus accosted me:

"'Hail, my brother indeed! Thou hast now become one of us. The environment is at thy command. Even life itself waits thy bidding. You are entitled to share with us whatsoever thy necessity may demand. As we help you, so will you help us. You will remain with us for a year. Then going out into the world, you will do the work appointed you, until such time *ah* one of the Circle of Isis dwelling within the Temple shall desire forever to lay aside the physical body. Then you will be permitted to enter our seclusion, never more to go hence, except in the prescribed way of all mortal-born. This will be at your option, years or centuries hence.'

"For one year, I dwelt quietly in the Temple, adding to my knowledge of the laws of the Universe. By practice increasing potency in the control of the inanimate, all the operations of nature became an open book. I comprehended, at last, the full scope of that dominion, which the spirit in its highest and best estate was intended by the Creative Thought to have, not only over the immediate environment, but in a larger sense to manifest in all the realms far or near. Wherever polarization and vibration are possible, and that is everywhere, there the thought currents reach the highest and the lowest, throughout the length and breadth of the Boundless.

"There had, now, also come to me distinct views on all subjects, so much so, that the Brothers in conversing with me, addressed me as on an equality with themselves, and my words were listened to, as having weight. It is one of their maxims, that to the new-born often come the clearest and brightest perceptions of wisdom.

"Thus passed the first year of my regenerated life, after being ' born again of water and the Spirit.' Bidding them all, at its end, a kind farewell, I made my way at once to the far East, being summoned thither by a swift messenger, to witness my wife and companion finally lay aside, for the accomplishment of present purpose, all earthly impediment.

"Since then I have visited every habitable quarter of the globe, and been brought into contact with all races of men in the practice of the healing art. In this, such wonderful power has been granted me by the Brotherhood, that I have been called a miracle-worker. This is true in the sense of doing wonderful things; but as out of the course and law of Nature, not so. Even the Causeless Cause cannot violate a law. Law is the sequence of Creative Thought. If one link in the chain were broken, then the whole structure must fall into destruction.

"Wealth has flowed in upon me, not because I needed it, but because it was necessary for those who needed healing, to make sacrifice to attain the thing they sought. Nine-tenths of all disease, is the result of selfishness, which paralyzes polarization, and neutralizes vibration, thus destroying the harmony in the working out of the Creator's designs. This must always be overcome, if we desire a radical cure. But the end of my wanderings, and my service as one of the world's workers is near at hand. Look!"

I glanced at my Master. His features had become set and forceful. His eyes were looking intently out into the far-off. As he stopped speaking, the ring on his finger blazed out like a meteor. The polished wall opposite reflected a mountain peak crowning a broken country. I knew it was the exterior of the Temple. The scene dissolved into magnificent and well-watered gardens. I recognized the fountain in the center, and the high precipices, ever keeping protecting watch.

A third time the view changed. Now it was an upper chamber, into which, through a many pillared colonnade, streamed the rays of the rising sun. In the center, lay a reclining form, while about him were grouped fourteen sages, old in appearance of body, but young in spirit, and in the inspiration that moved and controlled the outer. Numberless ages rested on them all. He who was at ease said:

"Brothers, my body has become only an encumbrance. I have finished that which I desired to do. If I find I so need, I can bring a fresher, newer mechanism, in which the spring of sequence is still uncoiled, to the service of the Brotherhood. I seek the invisible section, composed of those who, in perfected ripeness, have gone from us. By the absolute power of the Omnipotent word, I will ashes to ashes, and freedom from all its claims upon myself."

I could hear these words, like the murmur of the sea-shell, shaping itself into syllables. As he finished speaking, a form, luminous in its astral condensation, dilated above where the body had just lain. So much of the body itself had become purified and essential, and thus capable of being absorbed into the astral principle, that only a little outline of dust alone marked the place where but now the physical body had reclined.

The floating form turned its luminous countenance to the Master and beckoned. The word "Come," echoed in the air. The group of watchers in the form, turned their impressive, Messianic faces toward him, and their voices as one said, "Come!"

"At last," said the Master, "I am called. The purpose in giving you this history will develope. You will hear from me again." Rising, he took me by the left hand, and laid his right hand upon my head. A baptism as of fire, thrilled through my whole body. I felt myself drawn irresistibly toward the Brotherhood, wherever visible or invisible they might exist. With this parting benediction out of the Silence, he accompanied me to the outer door, and bade me farewell.

Not many days after, a letter requested me to call at the office of a well-known and respectable firm of solicitors in the City. Here I was presented with a deed of gift of all the property described and the appurtenances thereto, on the sole condition that I should take up my residence here. I accepted the trust. I have written this record in the room where it was given me. The luminous wall, sometimes by picture and sometimes by word, has ever and anon refreshed my memory. And now as I write the closing words, I, too, am waiting for the time when I may be admitted into full fellowship with the Brotherhood.